Amy Cross is the author of more than 250 horror, paranormal, fantasy and thriller novels.

OTHER TITLES BY AMY CROSS INCLUDE

1689
American Coven
Angel
Anna's Sister
Annie's Room
Asylum
B&B
Bad News
The Curse of the Langfords
Daisy
The Devil, the Witch and the Whore
Devil's Briar
Eli's Town
Escape From Hotel Necro
The Farm
Grave Girl
The Haunting of Blackwych Grange
The Haunting of Nelson Street
The House Where She Died
I Married a Serial Killer
Little Miss Dead
Mary
One Star
Perfect Little Monsters & Other Stories
Stephen
The Soul Auction
Trill
Ward Z
Wax
You Should Have Seen Her

ELECTRIFICATION
THE HORRORS OF SOBOLTON BOOK FIVE

AMY CROSS

This edition
first published by Blackwych Books Ltd
United Kingdom, 2024

Copyright © 2024 Blackwych Books Ltd

All rights reserved. This book is a work of fiction.
Names, characters, places, incidents and businesses are
the product of the author's imagination or are
used fictitiously. Any resemblance to actual persons,
living or dead, or to actual events or locations,
is entirely coincidental.

Also available in e-book format.

www.amycross.com
www.blackwychbooks.com

CONTENTS

CHAPTER ONE
page 15

CHAPTER TWO
page 23

CHAPTER THREE
page 33

CHAPTER FOUR
page 41

CHAPTER FIVE
page 49

CHAPTER SIX
page 57

CHAPTER SEVEN
page 65

CHAPTER EIGHT
page 73

CHAPTER NINE
page 81

CHAPTER TEN
page 89

CHAPTER ELEVEN
page 97

CHAPTER TWELVE
page 105

CHAPTER THIRTEEN
page 113

CHAPTER FOURTEEN
page 121

CHAPTER FIFTEEN
page 129

CHAPTER SIXTEEN
page 137

CHAPTER SEVENTEEN
page 145

CHAPTER EIGHTEEN
page 153

CHAPTER NINETEEN
page 161

CHAPTER TWENTY
page 169

CHAPTER TWENTY-ONE
page 177

CHAPTER TWENTY-TWO
page 185

CHAPTER TWENTY-THREE
page 193

CHAPTER TWENTY-FOUR
page 203

CHAPTER TWENTY-FIVE
page 211

CHAPTER TWENTY-SIX
page 219

CHAPTER TWENTY-SEVEN
page 229

CHAPTER TWENTY-EIGHT
page 241

CHAPTER TWENTY-NINE
page 249

CHAPTER THIRTY
page 257

ELECTRIFICATION

CHAPTER ONE

Today...

"WELL, IT'S... I DON'T exactly know what I'm looking at, but it certainly seems to be broken."

Standing way out past the forest to the north of the town, Sheriff John Tench looked at the tangled mess of metal that lay on the grass. A dozen engineers were already inspecting the scene, trying to work out what could have caused so much damage and how it could be quickly repaired, while John had sought the advice of Abe Landseer, the technician who'd been sent out to oversee the recovery operation.

"I should warn you," Abe muttered, "that this isn't going to be a quick fix."

"How much longer will the town be without power?" John asked.

"A day, at least."

"A day?" John replied, genuinely shocked by this revelation. "Are you sure it'll be that long?"

"We've got to erect a whole new pylon here," Abe told him. "Usually that'd take even longer, but we've already got everything we need. You're new round here, aren't you?"

John nodded as he saw more emergency vehicle arriving on the scene, bumping their way along the dirt road that led through the forest and out into the clearing.

"This isn't the first time a pylon in the Sobolton Line has been damaged," Abe explained. "It's not even the second. Seems to happen every decade or two. Something – and we're really not sure what, although we've got our suspicions – takes a periodic disliking to one of the pylons along this stretch and sets about whacking one of 'em down. This has been going on for as long as these pylons have been here."

John turned and looked at the row of pylons that extended far off past the edge of the forest.

"You hear stories about what could do it," Abe told him. "It's certainly no accident. Whatever attacks the pylons clearly intends to cause maximum damage."

"What kind of equipment would be required?" John asked. "How many people would it take?"

"Someone with the right kind of vehicle could do it," Abe opined. "Planning would be key. This kind of sabotage could be highly dangerous if done in the wrong way. You've got to understand, we're dealing with a hell of a lot of juice. There's enough electricity running along this network to fry a man until he's nothing more than a black mark on the ground. But this sabotage along here has been going on for so long, I can't help thinking that it's knowledge that has been passed from generation to generation."

"You think there's some kind of organized resistance to the pylons?" John asked. "Why? Who could possibly object to... electricity?"

"Beats me," Abe replied. "My job's just to fix it when it happens. I was part of the crew that dealt with the last sabotage, which must have been about twenty years ago. And back then I remember guys on the crew who talked about the previous time too. This particular line was put up around the time of the second war, and there's been trouble ever since. If you ask me, there's obviously someone around Sobolton – either in the town or in the forest – who really hasn't been happy about the pylons. They've been taking occasional potshots at them ever since."

"Okay," John muttered, "I'll see what I can find out. I'd appreciate it if your men could get the power turned back on as quickly as possible, though. We've got generators for essential services, but otherwise the town's in a bit of a mess without any power. And I don't think the situation's going to get any better."

***

"We've had people calling in all morning," Tommy said as he followed John across the parking lot, heading toward the station. "They just keep asking the same questions over and over again, about when the power's coming back on."

"All we can tell them is the truth," John replied. "There are people out there working on the situation as quickly as they can. I'm expecting the power to be back late tonight or perhaps early tomorrow morning. At least this didn't happen back when we had all that snow or ice."

"Do you think it could be something to do with cellphones?"

Reaching the bottom of the steps, John

turned to him.

"I've got a cousin out in Utah," Tommy continued, "and he says they're always having to deal with people smashing cellphone towers. It's to do with the waves, or the wires or the signals or something like that. I don't really understand, to be honest, but there are people out there who believe that the cellphone towers are somehow beaming stuff into their heads."

"Well," John said cautiously, "I don't know a great deal about that, but it's an electricity pylon that's been damaged, not a cellphone tower."

"So it can't be the same thing?"

"I don't think so," John muttered. "Still, I'm worried that whoever did this might strike again. Apparently the last act of sabotage against the power system was about two decades ago."

"I remember that," Tommy told him, before turning and looking over at the street. "It was eerie then, and it's eerie now. You don't realize how much of a hum there is in a place, not until that hum is gone. There's so much stuff that's always using up loads of power, and when they're all quiet..." He paused, and for a moment the two men simply stood and watched the row of stores opposite, and the diner a little further along. "It makes you realize how reliant you are on that sort of thing," he added.

"And how noisy the world usually is."

"It's only temporary," John pointed out. "The generators at the important sites should have no trouble keeping going for as long as they're needed. Obviously the lack of power is a setback and an inconvenience, but it's not like we've been knocked back to the Stone Ages. Not just yet."

"Doctor Law's furious," Tommy replied. "He keeps talking about cavemen and cannibalism, but to be honest I think he's just annoyed that he can't work the radio in his office."

"Then he should get one of those wind-up radios that I've been hearing about," John said with a faint, slightly amused smile, before turning and leading Tommy up the steps and through the station's front door. "There's no harm in being prepared."

"I guess I just don't like realizing how vulnerable we all are," Tommy admitted. "If the world beyond Sobolton suddenly stopped working, how long would we last? How would we get our food? How would we keep warm?"

They stopped at the desk, and Tommy turned to John.

"Did you hear that?" he asked.

"What?" John replied.

"Our footsteps." Tommy turned and walked

back to the doors and then over to John again. "They're kinda squeaky. You don't usually hear them because of all the electrical devices and stuff going on, but now it's so quiet..." He pushed a foot against one particular board on the floor. "This is a little bit loose," he continued. "Do you hear? It's like we're living in a different world."

"Think of it as a short vacation from how things usually are," John replied. "Try to make it fun."

"That's what I told Tracy and Josh," Tommy admitted. "I think they don't really mind today, but if this drags on for much longer, a lot of people in Sobolton are going to start panicking."

"Make a poster and stick it on the front door," John said, "telling people that the power's coming back on tomorrow. I was just out at the site and I saw all the work that's going on, I'm absolutely certain that soon everything's going to be back to normal." He sighed. "Of course, this *had* to happen just when I was making a possible breakthrough in the Little Miss Dead case. I was planning to really focus on that today."

"Sir?" Carolyn said, making her way back to the desk from the filing cabinet in the corner, "someone arrived to see you just now. I think he's in the bathroom, but he seemed kind of... keen."

"Did he give a name?" John replied.

"He was being a little evasive," she explained. "I don't think he's dangerous or anything like that, but I definitely got a strange vibe. I'm pretty sure he knows you."

Before John could reply, he heard the bathroom door opening. He turned to see a figure stepping out, and then he froze as soon as he spotted a very familiar face.

"Hey, Dad," Nick Tench said, stepping just a few feet away with a hint of a smile. "Good to see you again. You know, you can be a *very* difficult man to track down."

CHAPTER TWO

Twenty years earlier...

SITTING AT THE TABLE in her cramped little kitchen, Lisa stared at the solitary candle that flickered next to her closed laptop. With the power having been out for several hours now, she felt fairly sure that Sobolton was in the grip of one of its periodic blackouts, and she figured that the supply most likely wouldn't be restored until at least morning. She knew she should get some sleep, but at the same time her mind was racing.

"What did you want to hide from me?" she whispered, staring at the flickering flame.

"Well," her father Rod's voice replied, "what do you *think* I wanted to hide from you?"

"You sent me away," she reminded him. "You sent me to that awful place."

"Was Lakehurst really so bad?"

"Dad -"

"It seemed like a nice old building to me. Pleasant grounds. Decent facilities. Plus the staff seemed nice and -"

"The staff were awful," she said through gritted teeth. "At least half of them were complete psychopaths, they were way worse than any of the patients."

She paused for a moment, thinking back to the long, high-ceilinged corridors of Lakehurst, and the cold room with a simple metal bed. There had been something almost prison-like about the place, and some of her fellow patients had been terrifying. The doctors and orderlies, however, had been very strict, and a shudder passed through her bones as she remembered some of the whispered ghost stories she'd heard about the place.

"So is this the plan now? Are you going to blame all your problems on other people?"

"I want to know why you sent me there," she said firmly, "and what you were trying to get me to forget. It's coming back piece by piece, but I haven't got it all figured out just yet. I feel as if -"

Stopping suddenly, she thought for a

moment about how exactly she could get her father to admit the truth. Finally, however, she realized that the whole conversation was pointless.

"You don't know," she whispered, as the flame continued to flicker. "You're not really here. You're not a ghost, you're just a figment of my imagination. So you don't know anything that I don't already know, you're just a way for me to talk to myself. I just get the feeling that if I keep doing this, I'm going to obscure the truth even more. I need to push you away and focus on the memories that are just beneath the surface." She took a deep breath, and after a moment she realized that any sense of her father was now gone. "I met Michael again," she said softly. "I don't quite remember how, but..."

Her voice trailed off for a moment.

"It's coming back to me," she added, as the candle flickered a little more brightly. "I met him not long after the first time. I think... I think he came back to find me."

***

1984...

A solitary candle sat flickering on the windowsill as

Lisa stared out the window, watching the darkened garden.

"This is intolerable," Rod said as he stormed through from the equally dark hallway. "How much longer is this stupid outage going to last? I had to cancel all my appointments today, and now it's looking like I might have to cancel everything tomorrow as well. How am I supposed to reschedule it all? I can't just magic up extra hours over the next few days. There are operations I'm supposed to be performing and examinations and test results to read and people to talk to. I can't live like this!"

"It's the same for everyone, Dad," Lisa said, before looking down at the novel that so far hadn't really been holding her attention, even as the candle's light danced across the pages. "Why not take this opportunity to unwind a little? Didn't you hear me playing the piano earlier? I've taken this enforced break from modern technology as a chance to reconnect with a calmer world."

"I'm going to the bar," he muttered, turning and stomping back out to the hallway. "I'm going to reconnect with whatever they've got that's still cold."

"Will they even be open?" she called after him.

"McGinty's never shuts," he replied, and she could hear him slipping into his coat. "They didn't shut during any of the blizzards and they damn well won't shut now. Even if the pumps don't work, they'll have enough bottled beer to keep us all going, plus I'm sure there's a generator or two out the back of the place. Hopefully Joe's down there and he'll have some inside information about this whole mess. Lisa, stay here and don't go out for any reason, okay? I'm still angry about your last little stunt and I'm absolutely not in the mood for any more nonsense."

She opened her mouth to reply to him, but in that moment she heard the front door opening and then slamming shut again, followed by footsteps heading away from the house. Allowing herself the briefest of smiles, she couldn't help but feel that her father was overreacting just a little. Sure, they'd had to eat sandwiches for dinner and they'd been forced to move everything out of the refrigerator and try to preserve it all in buckets of ice outside, but in general she felt that the blackout was actually quite refreshing. For a few seconds she listened to the silence of the house and realized that this kind of silence was extremely precious.

She looked back down at the book again and read a few more lines, but she quickly realized that she'd read these same lines three times already. Closing the book with a sigh, she looked at the cover image showing a scantily-clad woman in the arms of a fanged figure; she'd been reading a lot of vampire books lately, which made a change from ghosts and other creatures, but she just wasn't feeling this particular story. Reaching over to the table, she picked up a copy of a new series she'd been meaning to try, about ice folk living far off in Europe, and then as she flicked through the pages she lazily glanced out the window.

In that moment she froze, as she saw that somewhere mixed in with the shows on the far wall, she could just about see the shape of a person.

"Michael?" she whispered, getting to her feet and hurrying to the back door, then pushing it open and stepping into the garden, still limping on her injured ankle. "Is that you?"

She waited, and although she couldn't be certain, she felt increasingly sure that this shadow looked exactly like the shadow he'd cast on his last visit. A moment later the shadow moved, and she realized that he was making the shape of a dog's head with his hands; she watched as the shadow changed a little, and she saw that in fact the shape looked a little more like a wolf.

Suddenly the shadow wolf tilted its head

and looked up, and Lisa heard a rather bad impression of a howling wolf. She couldn't help but laugh, and a moment later Michael stepped out of the shadows and into the moonlight.

"Still doing your little shadow puppets?" she asked.

"Sorry," he replied. "That one wasn't my best."

"No, I liked it," she told him, wanting to go over but feeling as if she should hold back, at least for now. The last thing she wanted was to seem too keen. "Why are you here?"

"I wanted to see whether you're alright."

"You mean after you abandoned me in the forest?"

"I didn't abandon you in the -"

He stopped suddenly.

"Well, I see what you mean," he continued. "I went to get help, actually."

"And then you just didn't make it back," she pointed out. "The wolves returned, though. I don't even know how I made it back to town. I think I must have struggled home and then I passed out."

"Or somebody carried you."

"Yes, but who could -"

In that moment, realizing what he meant, she couldn't help herself; she instinctively took a few steps forward onto the grass, and she to really force herself to keep from running straight over to him.

"Did you?" she asked cautiously.

"Did I what?"

"Did you carry me all the way home?"

"Maybe."

"And then you dumped me on the sidewalk?"

"I knew you were starting to wake up," he replied, "and I didn't really want you to see me. I thought that would raise more questions that I could have answered at the time. I'm sorry, I know that sounds vague, but I can't really explain it properly. At least, not right now. I'm glad to see that you're okay, though." He paused, before turning to walk away. "I'll leave you alone now."

"Wait!" she called out, hurrying over to him and grabbing his arm, forcing him to stop. "Can I see you again?"

"I don't know if that's a good idea."

"How about you let me make that decision?" she asked. "Relax, I'm not talking about a date or anything like that, I just think it'd be fun to hang out. Let's just keep away from wolves, okay?"

"You don't like them?"

"I think I've met more than my fair share for

a while."

Michael paused, clearly lost in thought, before nodding a little.

"Do you want to go for coffee?" she asked.

"Here?" he replied. "I mean... in town?"

"Isn't that where people *usually* go for coffee?" she continued, before sighing again. "But we don't know how long this blackout's going to last, so maybe it's not the best idea for tomorrow. We need to do something a little more low tech. How about meeting me tomorrow morning outside the town hall? I bet I can think of something fun by then."

"I don't know," he said cautiously. "I really just wanted to see that you're okay, and that your foot's fine, and -"

"Please?" she added, hating the pleading tone in her voice but unable to stop herself. "Come on, I'm not *that* annoying, am I? Can't we try to hang out at least once? Without wolves chasing us, I mean."

He opened his mouth to reply, but he still hesitated for a moment as if he was genuinely having to give the idea some proper thought.

"Tomorrow at midday," he agreed finally. "Outside the town hall."

"Do you promise you'll be there?"

"I promise," he replied. "But I should go now. Take care of your foot, or your ankle or whatever, and I'll see you soon."

"It's kind of my foot *and* my ankle," she told him as he turned and hurried away into the shadows, causing the bushes to rustle for a moment before silence fell once more. "See you tomorrow, Michael. I'm really looking forward to it."

CHAPTER THREE

Today...

"NICE OFFICE," NICK SAID as he stepped through the doorway and stopped to look around the room. "You're not doing too badly for yourself here in this little backwater town, huh? Looks like you've really landed on your feet, Dad."

Walking past him, John immediately began to tidy up the papers on his desk, taking a moment to make sure that they were all hidden from sight.

"What are you working on?" Nick asked, heading over to join him and looking down at some of the documents. "Is it some big local case? Let me guess, did someone steal a shovel? Did a cat get stuck up in a tree? Is -"

Before he could finish, he spotted one of the autopsy photos showing the dead little girl.

"Hey, is that -"

"This is all strictly confidential," John said firmly, sliding the photo into a file so that it could no longer be seen. "I keep my office locked when I'm not here, but I forgot just now that this was on the desk when I opened the door for you. Please don't ask me about cases, because I can't talk about them."

"But you've got something juicy, right?" Nick replied, stepping around to the other side of the desk and watching as his father continued to tidy the various items away. "So this Sobolton place seems a little.. quaint. And kind of out in the middle of nowhere. Is that why you chose to come here? Did you want to get away from the rest of the world? Because when I arrived this morning and got to the motel, I found that the place doesn't even have any electricity. How rundown does a place have to be, to basically have no power at all?"

"There's an outage," John replied, still not meeting his gaze.

"Evidently. But what -"

"I wasn't expecting a visit," John added, finally looking at him. "You could have called to let me know you were coming."

"You didn't exactly send me your new details," Nick reminded him. "It took me a while to find you."

"I would have gotten around to it," John replied. "Things have just been a little... busy since I arrived here. I didn't have time yet."

"Running around trying to solve murders, are you? Maybe this place isn't so different to New York after all. Did someone kill the little girl in that photo? What did they do to her? Did she get stabbed or -"

"What do you want, Nick?" John snapped suddenly, clearly struggling to control his anger.

For a moment, the two men watched one another in silence, each seemingly frustrated by how the other was acting. Father and son had certain physical similarities, but their personalities couldn't have been more different. Even now, John was glaring at his only child as if he fully expected a complete apology for... something, while Nick was struggling to hide a laugh that was always beckoned forward in the presence of any kind of seriousness. Somehow, impossibly, this silence managed to stretch even longer in a room that remained devoid of the usual hum of modern life.

"Listen," Nick said finally, "there's something I'd like to talk to you about. Can we meet later?"

"I'm very busy."

"I came all this way," Nick pointed out. "I tracked you down, which wasn't easy."

"Fine," John replied, "I'll meet you at the diner after work. It's across the street from here, you can't miss it. I can be there at six."

"Six it is," Nick muttered, before turning and heading to the door. "But let's meet at the bar instead. I saw a place a little way over called McGinty's, so I'll be there at six on the dot. I'm looking forward to it, Dad."

"Shut the door as you leave," John replied, already starting to rearrange the files again, determined to throw himself back into his work. He waited until he heard the door bump shut, and then he turned to make sure that his son was gone. Sighing, he leaned back in his chair and stared into space for a moment, trying to regain some sense of equilibrium.

After a few seconds he glanced over at his jacket, which was hanging near the door, and his gaze soon focused on one of the pockets.

***

"I mean, it's old," Robert pointed out, as he held the

scrap of fabric up to take a closer look. "It must be made from one of those damn plastics that never break down. If I had to guess, I'd say it was part of a coat or jacket of some sort."

"That's exactly what I think it is," John told him. "I know this isn't strictly part of your remit, but going through the usual channels would take too much time. Is there any chance you could slip it to someone and get them to run an analysis?"

"Sure," Robert replied, lowering the piece of fabric and starting to slip it into an evidence bag, "but what exactly are you expecting to find?"

"I want to know everything about it," John admitted. "I've had it for a while, to be honest I kept meaning to throw it out, but lately... I just think it might be worth a second look. Let's just say that the manner in which I found it has left me wondering whether I was led to it directly."

"Care to make that statement even *more* vague?"

"I'm considering a lot of options," John told him. "I'm... widening my scope."

"Do you really think the little girl's name is Eloise?"

"You saw the tag," John pointed out. "It fits perfectly."

"I've never met anyone named Eloise in

Sobolton," Robert muttered, before furrowing his brow. "No, I tell a lie. Rod Sondnes was married to a girl from out of town with that name."

"Rod Sondnes?" John replied. "Lisa's father?"

"Rod and Eloise both died a long while back," Robert explained. "I don't remember Eloise too well, but I remember she seemed nice enough. I'm trying to remember where she actually moved here from, and how and why, but I just can't quite recall. I'm sure it doesn't matter." He hesitated for a moment. "I've got to admit, it'd be nice to no longer have to refer to her as Little Miss Dead."

"I've run a trace on the name," John told him, "and I can't find any mention of a missing girl named Eloise who fits the bill. That doesn't necessarily mean it's wrong, though."

"You think she might have been living off the grid?"

"It's possible," John suggested.

He paused for a moment, thinking back to the moment when the dead little girl had appeared in his office. She'd been pointing toward the far end of the room, and at the time he'd assumed she was trying to get him to look at the bookshelves, but now he realized that his jacket might well have been nearby as well. He certainly had no intention of telling anyone about that encounter, mainly because he was worried he'd be seen as a lunatic, but he couldn't shake the sense that the girl had been trying to draw his attention to something. Was she in some way connected to the disappearance of Lisa Sondnes?

"John?"

"Hmm?"

"For a moment there," Robert continued, "you looked like you were in a world of your own. Is something wrong?"

"I'm just keen to get moving with this case."

"And nothing else?" Now Robert hesitated for a moment. "I heard that you had a visitor earlier. Sorry, you know I hate to gossip, but Carolyn said someone from out of town -"

"That's nothing," John said quickly, keen to shut down that aspect of the conversation. He turned and headed to the door, already trying to figure out his next step. "Let me know as soon as you have anything on that piece of fabric. Or on anything else, for that matter. We've finally got some momentum in this case and I sure as hell don't want to let that slip now."

"How about we discuss this over a beer?" Robert asked, but the only response was the sound of John's footsteps hurrying away along the corridor.

Left standing all alone, Robert furrowed his brow for a moment, puzzled by John's reaction. Finally he held the scrap of fabric up again, turning it around in the light as he tried to work out exactly where to get started. He was more than accustomed by now to John's slightly odd requests, but even by those standards the latest line of investigation seemed just a little unexpected. In fact, he couldn't really work out why anyone would be interested in a scrap of some old jacket, but he also knew that his job wasn't to ask questions about the investigation. That, he supposed as he turned and headed over to the desk, was for smarter men.

Still, as he set the piece of fabric down, he couldn't help but hesitate for a moment as he thought back to a day twenty years earlier.

"Lisa Sondnes," he whispered. "What *really* happened to you?"

CHAPTER FOUR

1984...

SITTING ON A WALL near the front of the town hall, bathed in morning light, Lisa swung her legs and looked along the road again. She knew she had no reason to worry just yet, but she'd arrived early for her meeting with Michael and she'd been hoping that he'd be early too. She couldn't shake a sense of nervousness, and the anticipation was clawing at the inside of her chest, but at the same time she also felt excited.

She looked both ways, still spotting no sign of him, and then she sighed yet again as she looked down at the grass.

"Busy morning?"

Turning to look over her shoulder, she saw

Joe Hicks making her way over.

"The glories of youth," Joe muttered with a leery grin. "I remember what it was like to have all the time in the world, and to be free to just sit around on my backside doing absolutely nothing."

"I'm waiting for someone," she said awkwardly.

"Oh, sure you are." He stopped and looked her up and down for a moment. "Hot date?"

"Just a friend."

"And would that be a friend of the male persuasion?"

Gritting her teeth, and hoping that Joe would get the message and simply walk away, Lisa made a point of looking once again along the road. She saw various people wandering past the row of shops, and a few familiar faces heading into the diner, but there was still no sign of Michael. Checking her watch again, she realized that he was now technically late.

"Your dad never told me that you had a boyfriend," Joe said.

"I don't."

"How's your ankle?"

"Fine."

"Still limping?"

"Don't you have somewhere to be?" she asked, finally letting her irritation boil over as she looked up at him. "Sorry," she added, aware that he could make her life difficult. "I'm just busy."

"You know," he replied, "you remind me of your dad a lot, but you also remind me of your mom. You've got that stubborn streak that Rod could never quite iron out of her. I used to joke about that, I used to tell Eloise that she reminded me of one of those cows that just refuses to go where it's told. There's no reason for it to be so intransigent, it just refuses to obey." He paused. "Do you know what intransigent means, Lisa?"

"I do."

"That's because you're a smart cookie," he continued, still fixing her with a determined stare. "Yeah, you're a *real* smart cookie." He paused again. "Lisa, when you were out in the forest and missing and all that, did you... see anything?"

"I saw a lot of trees."

"Huh," he chuckled. "Sure, but apart from that, did you see anything that struck you as being a little odd? 'Cause I still don't quite get what happened after your bike was run over and got all mangled."

"How do you know it got run over?" she asked.

"That's what you said, isn't it?"

"I said it got damaged by a car," she reminded him. "I didn't specifically say that it got run over."

"Well, I must have assumed," he told her,

before turning as one of the other officers yelled at him. "I've got to go, Lisa, but it's been nice talking to you. Now, if you remember anything you spotted out in the forest, anything you think might be worthy of further investigation, I want you to come and tell me." He paused for a few seconds, as if there was still something else he wanted to get off his chest. "Or if you met anyone," he added, "then that might be of interest too. We're still looking for a few people from the bus crash, so any clues would be highly valuable."

"I'm sorry," she replied firmly, "but I really don't think that I can help you."

"Joe!" the other officer shouted, waving at him from the window of a police cruiser parked nearby. "We've got to go!"

"See you around, Lisa," Joe muttered as he wandered away. "Don't go getting into any more trouble."

"Whatever," she said under her breath, as she checked her watch yet again. Looking along the road, she realized that Michael was now well and truly late. "Come on, where are you?" she whispered. "I want to hang out."

***

"Don't be silly," Rod said as he set a pair of used plastic gloves on the counter, "you know I always like it when you pop in to visit. What's up, Lisa? Are you already measuring the place up?"

"What do you mean?" she asked, picking up one of the scissor-like surgical implements on the side and taking a closer look.

"I mean that one day all of this will be yours," he continued. "Assuming you still want to study veterinary science, that is."

"Of course I do."

"You'll be really good at it, you know," he told her, unable to hide a faint smile. "I don't want to embarrass you, Lisa, but I'm pretty sure you'll be a chip off the old block and -"

"Why would someone not turn up for a date?" she asked suddenly, turning to him. Slightly shocked by her own question, she hesitated before shaking her head. "I'm sorry," she continued, "I don't know why I asked that. It's just that I don't understand why someone would agree to meet somewhere and then just not show up. Am I wrong, or is that incredibly rude?"

She waited for an answer.

"Did you say... date?"

"A meeting," she sighed. "Whatever. I shouldn't have said anything."

"So *that's* why you came to the office today," he said, nodding sagely as if he was finally starting to pull all the pieces of the puzzle together. "I thought it was a little odd that you showed up and didn't seem to have anything in particular to be doing. You were planning on meeting a boy."

"Can we drop it?"

"And he didn't show up, huh?" he continued. "Okay, well, that's pretty bad but you never know whether something unexpected came up. I was once two hours later to meet your mother for an early date, but when I got there she was still hanging around. She gave me hell for it, but I made sure I was never late again. So my advice would be to give this guy a second chance, but if he's late again then maybe he's not the best kind of guy. Do you see where I'm coming from?"

"The worst thing is that I feel like a complete idiot," she muttered. "I shouldn't care. It wasn't even a date, not really. We were just going to meet and hang out, that's all, and I definitely shouldn't be acting like it was important. I guess I just don't like the way I was left hanging around looking like a complete fool, and it didn't help that your buddy Joe Hicks showed up and started talking to me. I should never have even bothered, I should have known that it was just a set-up."

"There's nothing wrong with putting yourself out there a little," he pointed out. "In a careful way, obviously."

"There is if it makes you feel like this."

"No, I get it," Rod replied cautiously, "but to be honest, I think it's about time you went on a date." He wandered to another counter and began to fiddle with some instruments, although he was quite clearly just trying to act casual so that he could ask more questions. "So what's the lucky fellow's name?" he asked. "Where did you meet him? Is he a local boy? Hey, were you with him when you were missing? Because if you were, I'm not sure -"

"No!" she spluttered, fully aware that she'd talked herself into a mess. "Yes. I mean... no. Not really. Sort of. It's complicated, Dad."

"Of course it's complicated," he said. "Anything worthwhile always is."

"Can we just drop it?" she asked, heading to the door. "I don't want to talk about it. You wouldn't understand, anyway."

"Well, I dated a few times when I was younger," he pointed out. "I dated your mom, and that worked out pretty well, so my advice might not be all bad." He waited for a reply, but she was already out in the corridor, almost bumping into Hayley from the front desk as she hurried away.

"Is everything alright?" Hayley asked, stopping at the door. "Is Lisa upset about something?"

"Oh, she's *definitely* upset about something," Rod replied, unable to suppress a growing smile, "and everything's definitely alright. In fact, I think my little girl's finally starting to grow up and let herself get involved in this messy old world. And I absolutely couldn't be prouder."

CHAPTER FIVE

Today...

"SO I'M JUST SUPPOSED to... sit here?"

"I know this might not seem like a good use of your time," John replied, as he and Tommy sat in a police cruiser near Lisa's old apartment, "but right now I need somebody here that I can trust. Someone who won't sneak off to the store around the corner, or sit playing games on his phone and miss anything important."

"But... what exactly do you think I might see?" Tommy asked, peering out at the apartment building across the street. "Didn't you say that her place has been empty for years?"

"Exactly," John pointed out, "but I've got a feeling that for some reason, someone has been coming here regularly. I want to know who that person is."

"Do you think..."

Tommy's voice trailed off for a few seconds.

"Do you think that person might know what happened to Lisa Sondnes?"

"I really can't be sure," John replied, "but I'd like to find out." He checked his watch. "Remember, if you see someone, don't approach. Just try to get a photo of them, and then trail them if it's safe to do so. There's a chance I might have scared the suspect off already, but he might come back."

"And this is connected to the Little Miss Dead case?"

"I don't know," John admitted, before opening the door and climbing out of the cruiser. "Sometimes I worry that I'm making connections where there aren't any, but I really feel as if we're starting to get somewhere. We have a possible name for the girl, we have possible sightings of her in the forest on a night shortly before she died, and Doctor Law's working on a few other possibilities."

"Do you know when the power's likely to come back on?"

"I really hope it's by the end of today," John replied. "If people have to spend a second night without electricity, we might end up with a full-scale riot on our hands and -"

Before he could finish, his phone started buzzing. Slipping it from his pocket, he looked at the screen and saw that one of the guys from the office was trying to get through. He slammed the car door shut and tapped to answer the call, and then he turned to look once more at Lisa's apartment windows.

"Boss?" a voice on the other end of the line said cautiously. "Greg just gave up a tip. Someone took a vehicle in for repairs and... well, I think you might want to take a look at it."

***

"How many times do I have to tell you guys," Jerome said, his voice almost fizzing with frustration, "I didn't use it to ram anything! I woke up and my truck was missing, and then a buddy of mine called to say he'd spotted it out at Manor Ridge. I went over and sure enough, there it was, and the front was all smashed up. So I brought it in here. I didn't expect to have the cops called on me!"

"I was talking to some of the guys from the station this morning," Greg said, leaning against the wall, "and then when Jerome brought his truck in... I mean, it sure looks like it's been used to hit something, and I thought about what they were saying about the pylons."

"Mr. Richards," John said, looking over at

Jerome, "why didn't you call us to let us know that your vehicle was missing?"

"Because I found it before I had to," Jerome told him. "So I figured why bother with all the paperwork? It's not like you guys have a great track record when it comes to solves crimes round these parts."

"It's important that any crimes are recorded," John told him.

"I'm pretty sure your insurance company would want that," Greg muttered.

"Mr. Richards," John continued, "do you know exactly when your truck went missing?"

"Must've been after six last night," Jerome explained wearily, clearly not too interested in going into too much detail. "Do we really have to get into all this? Greg, you didn't need to call the cops into this situation."

Greg held his hands up, as if to indicate that he had no other option.

"So it could well have gone missing a few hours before the pylon was damaged," John suggested.

"There's grass and mud on the tires," Greg observed, nodding toward the truck. "That thing's definitely been driven off-road."

"Not by me!" Jerome said firmly.

"Nobody's accusing you of anything," John replied, "but if your vehicle has been used in a criminal act, then your cooperation would be greatly appreciated."

"But would a truck be able to knock out a pylon?" Greg asked. "I'm no expert, but that sounds unlikely."

"That's a good point," John told him. "This whole situation feels needlessly theatrical to me, as if somebody's hell bent on making us pay attention to what happened out there. Cutting the power for the town is just one part of their plan. They want us to realize that they're out there. They want us to pay attention to them."

"They want us to know what they can do to us," Greg suggested.

John turned to him.

"It's like a warning, right?" Greg continued. "They know we can fix the pylon, just like we fixed the damage after all the other blackouts over the years. They want us to know that they can do this whenever they feel like it. They're showing us that they have the upper hand."

"Who are *they*?" Jerome asked.

"I wouldn't like to make any comment on that," Greg admitted, before glancing at John. "You're still an outsider, Sheriff Tench," he added. "There have been stories for years about things that live out there in the forest. They keep away from us and we keep away from them, and there's only ever trouble when the two worlds mix. If you ask me, by damaging that pylon, someone was trying to send us a message. They're interfering with us because they think we interfered with them."

"And how exactly would we have done that?" John asked.

Greg opened his mouth to answer, before hesitating for a moment. The lights briefly flickered, hinting at a restoration of power, before falling dark again.

"Almost," Greg said with a sigh. "Better luck next time, huh?"

"I need to call my wife," Jerome muttered, taking his phone out of his pocket as he headed to the door. "My battery's not going to last much longer. If the power's not back on soon, everyone's gonna run out of battery and then we won't even be able to call each other. Think about that!"

"Something's different out there, John," Greg said after a few seconds, lowering his voice a little as if he preferred to not be overheard. "I can't put my finger on it, but I spend a fair bit of time hunting. I don't know what it is, but a while back – around the time you arrived, actually – the air seemed to change."

"The air?"

"Or something *in* the air," he continued, before shaking his head. "I don't know, I'm sounding like a total idiot, but I swear it happened. It's like some invisible balance got upset and... I can't see what happened but I can see the aftereffects of it. Everyone can, on some level, even if they're not quite sure how to express it. The whole town's on edge and it's not just because of Little Miss Dead." He paused again. "But it sure as hell started right around the time you found her in the ice."

"Can you examine this truck more carefully?" John asked, preferring to avoid any discussion that might veer into the esoteric. "Can you try to find some scraps of paint, or something else that we can use to link it to that pylon?"

"Most of my tools are out of action until the power comes back," Greg admitted, "but I can certainly get started with a few things."

"I'm also going to send some guys through to swab down the inside of the truck," John told him. "I want to know who took this thing. And I'm going to see if any people living near Mr. Richards might have cameras on their doors, anything that might have caught what happened. In fact, I think I might head up there right now and go door to door."

"Wow," Greg replied.

"Wow?"

"I guess I'm just not used to dealing with a sheriff who actually gets off his butt and puts in the leg work," he replied as he wandered over to the truck and took another look at the damage to the front. "Especially when it comes to the forest. Let me tell you, if Joe Hicks – bless his rotten soul – was still in charge, this whole thing would be getting swept under the rug. You're a real breath of fresh air, John. I've got a feeling you might actually get to the bottom of what's really been going on!"

CHAPTER SIX

1984...

"SO YOUR NEXT QUESTION, and remember that this is for ten thousand dollars, is on the subject of -"

Before the game show host could say another word, Lisa pressed the button on the front of the television set, switching it off so that she could finally escape the babbling noise. Since getting home from her father's office, she'd tried everything she could think of to calm her racing mind; usually she could simply get back into a novel, but this time she found that she could barely sit still, and daytime shows hadn't helped either. Now, as she walked to the window and looked out at the garden, she felt a growing sense of anger as she realized that Michael had simply not bothered to show up for their meeting.

She knew her father wouldn't want her using the generator to run the television, but in that moment she didn't care.

"How dare you?" she whispered, unable to stay calm for even a moment longer as she thought about Michael's failure to appear. "How rude can one person be?"

She watched the wall at the far end of the garden, and she wondered whether – come nightfall – she might see another of Michael's little shadow shows. Part of her wanted to wait and then pointedly ignore him, but at the same time she was already thinking about that strange little cabin out in the forest, and part of her wanted to head straight over there and let Michael know that she was highly unimpressed. The idea was utterly foolish, of course, because she knew there might well be more wolves out there, but at the same time she knew that her father occasionally went on hunting trips with friends, and he was always safe because he carried proper protection.

And if *he* could do that, then why couldn't she?

***

Opening the cabinet, Lisa took out one of the rifles

her father often took out to the forest. She knew the basics of how to operate a gun, although deep down she still wondered whether she was actually going to go through with this plan.

She grabbed a box of ammunition, only to see that these particular bullets were silver-tipped. Not wanting to use anything expensive that her father might miss, she pulled out another box of more regular bullets, and she began to load a whole bunch into her backpack.

"This is the stupidest thing you've ever done," she said out loud, trying to talk herself out of what she knew was a flash of childish irresponsibility. "You're better than this. You've always prided yourself on being smart, you've always made fun of people who act rashly, and this would be a really bad time to break the habit of a lifetime."

Closing the backpack, she hauled it over her shoulder before turning to head to the door, only to wince as she felt another twinge of pain in her injured ankle. Looking down, she realized that while the wound was healing, any attempt to hike through the forest would undoubtedly make it bad again. She took a deep breath, wondering whether she could still find some way to push on, and then finally she dumped the rifle and the backpack on the table and sat herself down in one of the chairs.

"Fine," she said with a heavy sigh, "I might

be an idiot but I'm not *that* stupid. I wouldn't even know exactly where to find the damn cabin, anyway." She looked at the rifle and felt a rush of relief as she realized that sanity had prevailed. "Sorry, Michael," she added under her breath. "I'm not going to put my life in danger – again – just to tell you that you're a rude, arrogant asshole."

***

"Well, the power's still off," Rod said, flicking the switch on the wall yet again as if he expected to suddenly have some luck. "Looks like we're in for a second night like this."

"We've got a load of candles," Lisa pointed out, sitting on a chair in the corner of the room as she tried to focus on her book. A candle was burning on the table next to her. "I think we'll survive."

"I spent the day cleaning at the office," Rod muttered, "but if I have to cancel tomorrow's work as well, I'm going to start running into serious difficulties." He flicked the switch again, then again, and then several more times. "How's a man supposed to -"

"Flick that switch one more time," Lisa hissed suddenly, "and I'll scream!"

With his finger poised to do just that, Rod opened his mouth to protest before realizing – at the very last second – that his daughter just might not be kidding. He looked around for a few seconds as if searching for something to say, and then he cleared his throat before heading to the door.

"I don't like blackouts, that's all," he muttered. "I don't like anything that stops me working. I get fidgety, and when I get fidgety, my thoughts run all wild and crazy. I just like to keep my life organized."

"I'm sure it'll all be fixed soon," she told him.

"That's what I've been telling myself all afternoon," he called back to her as he carefully made his way across the pitch-black hallway, heading toward the stairs. "The longer it goes on, though, the more I can't help but worry. I've already started planning how to move all the furniture around at the office. Can you believe that? If we get another day like today, I might actually start doing something so stupid! And don't think you're safe, either, because I'll drag you in and make you help with the painting!"

"Painting?" she replied.

"Oh, there'll be painting," he told her. "If we don't have power tomorrow morning, there'll be more painting than you can possibly imagine!"

She could hear him still muttering away to himself upstairs, no doubt complaining about the power outage as if it might be some kind of plot directed at him personally, but she couldn't help smiling as she realized that her father was being driven just a little bit out of his mind. She looked down at her book, still smiling, but after a moment she realized that she really wasn't in the mood to keep going with the tale of a young woman falling in love with a vampire. Closing the paperback, she stared at the lurid cover image depicting a maiden wearing a nearly transparent gown collapsing into the arms of a muscle-laden man who looked absolutely nothing like the vampire in her head. The more she stared at the picture, however, the more Lisa realized that everything about the book was completely unrealistic.

"This is the 1980s," she muttered under her breath, "not the 1880s. We're a little more modern than that and -"

Before she could finish, she heard something bumping against the window. She turned and looked, but all she saw was darkness outside. Still, she couldn't shake a flicker of concern, so she got to her feet and walked over to the door; once she'd double-checked that the lock was secure, she cupped her hands around her eyes so that she could peer out a little better at the garden. Although she was trying to tell herself otherwise, she knew that deep down she was clinging to the hope that Michael might appear with some crazy excuse to explain his non-appearance earlier. She told herself that she wasn't going to accept any dumb explanations, that he'd really have to work to win her over again, but she also knew that there was one glaring reason for her attitude on this matter.

She felt hurt.

Hurt that he'd stood her up, and hurt that he apparently didn't care enough to even send a message. Sure, he might be busy, but he could at least let her know that he was sorry. Eight hours after they were supposed to meet, nothing short of a massive disaster should have been able to stop him.

Not if he cared.

Which he clearly didn't.

"Asshole," she muttered, watching for a moment longer to make absolutely sure that there was no-one outside, then drawing the drapes and blowing out the candle, then heading to the door. "See if I care. You can come rocking up with any excuse you like, but it won't wash. I'm done."

As she made her way carefully up the staircase, the back room was left bathed in darkness and silence. Nothing moved at all, although after a moment a very faint scratching sound could be heard coming from outside; the sound continued for a few more seconds before fading away, and now the room was once again completely undisturbed. This remained the case for the next few minutes, and then the next few hours, well past midnight and on into the small hours of the morning.

Eventually a crack of moonlight broke through a gap in the drapes, catching the front cover of Lisa's book, picking out the garish image of a damsel in distress and her unlikely supernatural hero.

CHAPTER SEVEN

Today...

"RACCOONS," JACQUES FERRER MUTTERED as he hobbled through to the study at the rear of his house. "That's why I got it. Damn things keep going through my trash and I wanted to catch 'em in the act."

"I see," John replied politely, having to duck his head down slightly as he followed Ferrer through the slightly low doorway.

"Of course, I don't know what I was gonna do once I had 'em on tape," he continued, pulling an office chair out and then slumping down on the seat so that he could pull his computer keyboard closer. "It's not like you could arrest them, but I wanted to see the critters."

"Yeah," John said, struggling to know how to respond to Ferrer's long-winded tales.

"So I installed the camera, and it's got a great view of my trashcans, but it also covers Jerry's place opposite. Gives me a real good view of his driveway." He logged onto the computer and started bringing up the feed from the camera on his front door. "I always like to joke with him and tell him that any time he has a lady visitor over, I'll be able to see when she arrives and when she leaves. The camera's motion-activated, you see, and it's sensitive enough that it records even when someone's out the front of Jerry's place."

"I appreciate you taking the time to look through the footage," John replied. "As I mentioned, we're really just -"

Stopping suddenly, he furrowed his brow.

"Generator," Ferrer replied, as if he'd read his mind. "Got it running out back. It comes on automatically when there's a power outage. Hell, I barely even notice when anything like that happens. I need to stay connected, you see." He patted the top of the monitor as if it was some kind of pet. "If I went offline for any extended period of time, my buddies around the world would start to worry. We've got a league going, you see, and they couldn't get much work done without me." He paused. "Sheriff Tench, do you play any kind of online games?"

"I can't say that I do," John admitted.

"You should give it a try if -"

"Mr. Ferrer," John added, interrupting him, "I'm sorry to rush you, but I'm afraid that I don't have much time."

"*Call of Duty*," Ferrer told him. "I think a man like you, who has to carry a gun all the time, would be pretty damn good at a game like that. You should give it a try, it might even improve your reflexes and make you a better shot."

"Mr. Ferrer," John replied, "would you mind checking your footage for me?"

"Always glad to be of service," Ferrer replied, using the mouse to click on a folder on the screen, then peering at the various files inside. "They're all timestamped, of course," he muttered. "Ah, we've got something here. Something triggered the cameras around ten last night." He clicked to start the video, which began playing on the screen, showing a view of the trashcans on his driveway. "Is this what you wanted?"

"It might well be," John said, leaning down to get a better look. He could see Jerome's driveway in the video, with the truck parked just off the street. "What kind of -"

Before he could finish, he saw something moving in the video, and he watched as a raccoon climbed onto one of the trashcans in the foreground of the shot.

"See?" Ferrer exclaimed excitedly. "I told you!"

"Do you have any other videos from last night?" John asked, trying to hide a slight sense of irritation.

"Let's see," Ferrer replied, closing the video and then clicking on another. "This was about half an hour later. It's probably just raccoons again, though."

The second video started, but no raccoons were visible, although the trashcans had now been knocked over. On the far side of the street, however, three men had stepped into view and appeared to be slowly approaching Jerome's truck.

"Now, what do you think they're up to?" Ferrer murmured, leaning closer to the screen. "I'm sure it's nothing good."

John watched as one of the men fiddled with the truck, quickly managed to get its door open.

"They're pretty brazen, doing it in the open like that," Ferrer pointed out. "Sure, it was dark, but they must have realized that someone'd see them."

"I think that might be the whole idea," John replied, watching as two of the men climbed into the truck while the third remained on the street. "They wanted us to see them doing this. They wanted us to know that they don't care, it's some kind of -" He watched as the third man turned to look toward the camera. "Freeze it right there!"

Ferrer clicked to freeze the video.

"Can you zoom in?" John asked.

"I can try," Ferrer explained, "but the resolution'll get a little choppy. This is one of the best cameras on the market but it's got its limitations."

He enlarged the image, focusing on the third man, finally bringing the face into view and revealing what appeared to be a dark mark or hole covering the left eye.

"What do you make of that?" he asked. "Is it... I'm not expert, but it looks like that man's hurt. It looks like he hasn't got much left of one of his eyes."

***

"Nothing so far," Tommy said over the phone, as John sat in his cruiser outside Ferrer's house. "How much longer do you want me to stay here?"

"I'll send someone to relieve you around five," John replied, still looking at the print-outs he'd obtained from Ferrer's camera footage.

"Are you planning on having someone here all night?" Tommy asked.

"If that's what it takes."

John turned to another of the print-outs, which showed the three men driving the truck away. A moment later, however, he heard a loud crunching sound coming from the phone.

"Tommy?"

"Sorry," the other man replied, seemingly speaking with his mouth full. "I just needed some potato chips to keep me going. Hey, I know this is an official stakeout, but would it be okay if I nip into town and grab something to drink? I'll only be half an hour."

"I want you to stay there," John said firmly. "I know this must be boring for you, Tommy, but I need to know if anyone goes back to Lisa's apartment."

"But why would they?"

"I don't know, but Joe Hicks cared enough to keep the place empty. There has to be a reason for that." He looked at another of the print-outs. "Tommy, you've lived here all your life. Do you know anyone in Sobolton who has an injured left eye? It might be something recent, but it might also be an older wound."

"An injured eye?"

"They could have lost it in an accident," John suggested, "or perhaps they were born with some kind of problem."

"I can't think of anyone."

"Something like this would be pretty noticeable," John continued. "If it was a recent injury, I'm surprised the guy was walking around."

For a moment he thought back to the pack

of wolves that had attacked Joe Hicks. One of those wolves had been carrying an injury to its left eye, and although he knew there couldn't be an actual connection, John couldn't help but note the coincidence. For some reason that he wasn't yet able to fathom, many elements of these various cases all seemed to point back in one way or another to the wolf population that officially wasn't even supposed to exist out in the forest.

"Do you think the diner would deliver?" Tommy asked finally.

"Deliver what?" John asked.

"Coffee. Man, I know it's kinda pathetic, but you have no idea how much I need -"

"I'll bring you a coffee," John replied, cutting him off. "I'll swing by the diner and bring it straight over, okay? I'll even pick up something for you to eat."

"Are you sure? Boss, I don't want you to go to any trouble."

"It's fine," John said, checking his watch. "It's getting late, it's almost five. I'll bring your coffee and then I'll head back to the station. I've got a feeling I'm going to have to pull an all-nighter. Hopefully soon the power'll come back on, though, because -"

At that moment his phone began to beep, indicating that he had another call.

"Hold on," he added, before accepting the

call. "Sheriff John Tench here, what -"

"Mr. Tench," the tense voice on the other end of the line said before he could finish, "this is Abe Landseer out at the pylon in the valley. Listen, I think you'd better get out here with some of your men pretty damn fast. And bring an ambulance too. We've got a situation."

CHAPTER EIGHT

1984...

"DO YOU THINK IT'S too pink?" Rod Sondnes said, stepping back from the wall in the reception area and furrowing his brow. "Damn it, now that I've started, I think it might be too pink."

"So what do you want to do?" Lisa asked, stepping through into the room for a moment, dressed in old clothes that were already dappled with paint splatters. "Start again? Dad, we've already done a lot this morning and -"

"No, we can't start again," he sighed, interrupting her as he checked his watch. "It's almost ten. Do you think they'll have the power back on by lunchtime?"

"I really don't know," she told him.

"I'm sick of this," he muttered, grabbing his brush and getting back to work, painting the wall pink. "How long does it take to fix a power line, anyway? I really don't get what's taking these idiots so long, Lisa. I'll tell you what it is, they're probably paid by the hour so they'd rather sit around on their asses and drag the whole thing out another day. Don't they realize that our lives are pretty much at a standstill right now? I can't run my veterinary office without power, and most of the businesses in town are in the same boat. It's like we're... frozen."

"I'm going to go to the store," Lisa said, setting her tin of paint down and stepping carefully over the old newspapers covering the floor. "Do you want anything?"

"I want electricity!"

"Everyone wants electricity," she told him. "I need something to eat, and maybe a drink as well. I'll be back soon, and hopefully by then you've figured out what color you want me to paint the walls in the corridor." She opened the door before stopping to look back at him. "Pink works."

"It does?"

"It does," she said, nodding sagely. "Don't keep stopping and having doubts, Dad. You've made your decision. Now you need to stick to it."

***

"I had to throw everything from the chiller cabinet out," Dan Ward complained, leaning against the counter in his convenience store. "Can you imagine the waste? And people keep buying up all the toilet paper I have on the shelves. What's that all about? Why does a power outage make them want toilet paper? What exactly do they think is gonna happen?"

Allowing herself a faint smile as she continued to listen to the conversation, Lisa made her way along the aisle and looked at the rather bare shelves. She wasn't really hungry, but she'd felt compelled to get away from the office for a few minutes, if only to escape from her father's incessant complaints. Now, as she crouched down and looked at some bags of potato chips, she felt as if the power outage was dragging on for too long, even for her liking. Glancing up, she saw the lights on the ceiling and gave them a chance to come back to life.

Nothing.

"George and Lee have gone out hunting again," the woman at the front of the store complained. "They figure they might as well keep active while they can't get any work done. To be honest, I actually thought about joining them."

"If this keeps up, I might just close the store," Dan admitted. "I just get kinda antsy when I see so many gaps. There's a delivery due tomorrow, and it's too late for me to cancel the stuff that needs to be kept frozen or chilled. I don't know what to do, Emma, it's like the whole of civilization is collapsing."

"Things aren't quite *that* bad," Lisa muttered under her breath, as she grabbed a bag of chips and got to her feet. "Yet."

"George and Lee saw this very strange man out in the forest yesterday afternoon," the woman continued as Lisa stepped around into the next aisle. "Apparently they saw this young man, maybe twenty years old or so, stumbling through the bushes with all these cuts and bruises."

Lisa reached for a bottle of soda, before stopping as she caught up with the words she'd just heard.

"They called out to him," the woman explained, "but he barely even noticed them. According to George, the guy was looking pretty bad, like he'd been in a fight. He was wearing all black, and his clothes were kinda torn, and he was clearly in pain. He was clutching his side, but he didn't even slow down when George and Lee tried to help him."

Already realizing that her heart was racing, Lisa told herself that she had no way of knowing the identity of the injured guy in the forest. At the same time, the very basic description offered so far certainly sounded a lot like Michael.

"You get some weird ones out there occasionally," Dan sighed.

"They followed him for a little while," the woman said. "He was heading up northwest past Cutter's Hill, at least that's what they told me, but I don't think it makes sense that anyone would be going that way, because what's out there? There's nothing!"

Trying to put the pieces together, Lisa thought back to her journey through the forest. She couldn't be absolutely certain, of course, but she felt sure that anyone heading northwest from the area around Cutter's Hill would inevitably end up roughly in the vicinity of Michael's cabin. No matter how hard she tried to tell herself that there was no reason to worry, she was already starting to wonder whether some kind of injury might have kept Michael from meeting her the previous day.

Finally, unable to hold back, she hurried around to the front of the store.

"Excuse me," she said as soon as she saw the woman at the counter, "but exactly what time did your husband see this guy?"

"Just after lunch, I think," the woman replied, clearly puzzled by the interruption. "Why? Do you think you know who he was?"

"How long did they follow him for?"

"Just a little while," she admitted, glancing briefly at Dan before turning to Lisa again. "I think they just gave up when it became clear that he didn't want any help. I'm sorry, I don't mean to be rude, but why are you so interested? If you know something, you should go to the sheriff's office and report it."

"Yeah, I'll do that," Lisa said, before setting the chips down and hurrying out of the store, only to stop on the sidewalk as she realized that she couldn't possibly go to the police.

For a moment she felt as if the world was spinning all around her, as if the sidewalk was starting to tip her over, but she couldn't help thinking about Michael out there in his cabin. All morning she'd been trying to put him out of her thoughts, while managing a simmering sense of anger and rehearsing exactly what she'd say to him if he showed his face again. She'd come to the conclusion that he must have simply not bothered meeting her, that the whole thing had been some kind of joke, but now she realized that something serious might have happened.

"Tomorrow at midday," she remembered him saying a couple of nights earlier. "Outside the town hall."

"Do you promise you'll be there?" she'd replied, and now she realized just how desperate she might have sounded.

"I promise," he'd insisted. "But I should go now. Take care of your foot, or your ankle or whatever, and I'll see you soon."

Those words played over and over in her mind now, filling her thoughts until she realized that she could no longer bear the uncertainty. The thought of Michael struggling through the forest, perhaps injured by the same wolves that had attacked her on two separate occasions, sent a chill through her bones and in that moment she knew that she had no option other than to make sure he was okay. Sure, the guy seen by the hunters might have been someone else entirely, although in her mind's eye she could only see an image of Michael – bloodied and injured – struggling desperately to get back to the cabin. She imagined him all alone out there, suffering and perhaps even dying, and she felt as if she simply had to check on him.

Hurrying back to the office, she could barely think straight as she opened the door and looked inside to see her father still staring at the paint on the wall.

"There you are," he said with a heavy sigh. "Listen, I've been thinking -"

"I have to go!" she blurted out. "Sorry, Dad, I'm not sure how long I'll be. I might not be back until tomorrow."

"But what -"

Not even waiting for him to finish that sentence, Lisa turned and hurried away across the parking lot. She could see the forest in the distance, waiting beyond the limits of the town, and she couldn't shake a sense of panic that something might be really wrong with Michael.

CHAPTER NINE

Today...

"IT'S FINE," THE MAN said, wincing a little as he moved the towel away from his arm, revealing the thick cuts running up to his elbow. "Look, it's nothing. It's not broken. I'll be fine."

"We're going to take you to the hospital as a precaution," the paramedic told him. "This looks nasty, and you're going to need a tetanus shot."

"It didn't bite me!"

"Just to be safe," she continued, before helping him up from the canvas chair. "You're not going to argue with me and make this difficult, are you? How about you just agree to be a good patient, and then this'll all be over a lot quicker? Can you do that?"

"You're lucky I haven't pulled my men out already," Abe said firmly, watching as the guy allowed himself to be led to the back of a waiting ambulance. "I'd have every right to do that, you know. You can't expect us to work in dangerous conditions."

"I know," John replied, "but -"

"The damn things came out of nowhere!" Abe hissed. "A whole bunch of wolves, half a dozen of the damn things! At first we were kinda laughing and joking about them, but after a while I got to finding it spooky how they just seemed to be watching us all the time. Then one of the guys noticed they were spreading out a little, and I couldn't shake the feeling that they were starting to form a circle around where we were working. They were still keeping their distance, but after a while it wasn't a joke anymore."

"Did you provoke them in any way?" John asked.

"Are you kidding me? We were just getting on with things. Hell, we were making good progress until Johnny went to grab something from one of the trucks. He headed round to the back, I didn't think anything of it and then suddenly he cried out. One of those goddamn wolves had made a lunge at him and tried to bite him. The rest of us ran down there hollering and making as much noise as we could, and we chased the damn thing off, but not before it got Johnny with its claws." He turned and looked past the damaged pylon, as if he was still worried that there might be some wolves nearby. "They scattered after that, but I can tell they're still out there somewhere. I can feel it in my bones."

"I don't see any wolves now," John pointed out.

"The issue is that I'm responsible for the safety of my team," Abe said firmly as the ambulance began to drive away, ferrying the injured man to the hospital. "That means that if I'm concerned, I have every right to pull us out of here, and then you won't be getting your power back any time soon. So as the sheriff of this backward little place, it looks like you're gonna have to come up with some way to keep us safe."

"I'll have a couple of armed men here around the clock," John told him. "If those wolves come back, you'll be protected."

"There were at least half a dozen of them," Abe replied. "Do you really think two men'll be enough if they return?"

"I'll take charge of the operation personally," John said, checking his watch. "Soon it'll start getting dark, so I want to get them into position as quickly as possible. Would I be right in thinking that you're going to have to work into the night?"

"I want to make one thing very clear," Abe

continued. "I'm not happy about this situation. Not happy at all. And once we're out of here, I'm going to be putting in a formal report to my boss about the conditions we've been forced to work in. I've got one man out sick now with cuts from a wolf attack. If we so much as see the bastards again, I'll be pulling us all out and you guys in Sobolton can get used to a new life without electricity. Have I made myself clear?"

***

"Here?" Toby said, sounding a little concerned as he stood at the edge of the forest and looked into the darkness between the trees. "All night?"

"All night," John replied firmly. "At least until the team's finished working on the pylon and we've got the power restored. Once that's done and they leave, you can leave too, but until then I want both of you to stay in place. And if you see wolves coming close, you have orders to shoot."

"But there aren't any wolves round here," Sheila added. "Are there?"

"The jury's out on that for now," John told her. "Listen, I know this isn't ideal. I wouldn't pull you off leave and ask you to do this unless it was important. There's a man in the hospital right now with scratches all over his arm and his neck, and I'm sure I don't have to remind you that the whole town needs the power supply back up and running."

"Sure," Sheila said cautiously, "but... wolves?"

"You've got your rifles," John pointed out, as a cold wind blew in across the darkening space. "I've also brought out some extra portable lights with fully charged batteries, and I'm confident those should scare any local wildlife away. This is very much a precautionary move at this point in time. If you become at all concerned, call the station immediately and I'll have every available unit out here as quickly as possible."

"What about Tommy?" Toby asked.

"Tommy's working another case for me," John replied.

"I heard you've got him staking out the old Lisa Sondnes place," Toby continued, glancing briefly at Sheila before turning to John again. "I know it's not my place to bring this up," he added, "but... I don't know, people are starting to wonder why you'd be doing that. Boss, Lisa Sondnes disappeared twenty years ago, before most of us were even in long pants."

"Have you made a development in the case?" Sheila asked.

"Let's just say that I'm pursuing multiple avenues of investigation," John replied, keen to avoid getting into too many details. "Some of them might lead absolutely nowhere, but there's only one way to find out."

"What about Little Miss Dead?" Sheila continued. "I heard -"

"Let's focus on one thing at a time," John said, interrupting her. "Please, just keep these good folks safe while they finish working on our power supply. There'll be time for other discussions later." With that, he turned and headed toward the pylon, determined to end any conversation about other cases. Already, he felt as if the constant barrage of questions hinted at an underlying level of suspicion concerning his abilities as sheriff.

By the time he reached the pylon, he'd already made up his mind to go briefly back to town and get some rest, and then to join the team guarding the site. He knew that he needed to show the others they weren't alone.

"How's it going here?" he asked as he approached Abe.

"We're getting there," Abe replied, "but you should tell your people that they won't be getting their power back for a good few hours yet."

"Something made a real mess out here, huh?"

"You want to know what I think?" Abe asked, as they both looked up toward the top of the pylon high above. "I think someone really set out to cause the maximum possible disruption. Sure, that might be an accident, but something doesn't pass the sniff test for me. They knew exactly where to hit this thing, and they targeted it in a way that's left us really struggling to pull it all back together. Can you think of any reason why anyone might want to sabotage the Sobolton power supply like this?"

"I can't," John admitted, watching as two men worked at the very top of the pylon.

"Well, you'd better get your thinking cap on," Abe told him. "There's mile after mile of unprotected infrastructure out here, passing right through the forest. There's no way anyone can guard all of that, so if someone really wants to cause damage, I'm not sure how you'd stop them. The point I'm trying to make, Sheriff Tench, is that there are something like a hundred vulnerable pylons in this stretch alone. So what's stopping someone from waiting until we're out of here and then doing the same thing a few miles in either direction?"

"That would certainly be a problem," John pointed out, "but who -"

Before he could finish, they both heard the sound of a wolf howling somewhere in the distance. They turned and looked over toward the forest, where Toby and Sheila made for a rather uninspiring line of defense as they stood with their rifles. The howling sound had already faded to nothing, but the sky was darker still and a first quarter moon was coming into view above the mountains.

"You'll find the answers you seek," John heard Amanda Mathis saying, her voice echoing through his memories, "but you don't have all the time in the world. You need to find her before the next full moon."

"First things first," he told Abe, determined to deal with the power problem and then move on to all the other issues on his plate. "I'll be back in a few hours. One way or another, we have to get the power back on. I really don't think the people of Sobolton can handle another full night in the dark."

CHAPTER TEN

1984...

AS SOON AS SHE pushed the cabin door open, she saw him.

Michael was on the floor in the corner, wearing his usual black clothes but with obvious injuries all over his body. Setting her rifle and backpack down, Lisa raced over to him and dropped to her knees; she was hugely relieved to find that he was still alive, but she couldn't help noticing that he seemed groggy and a little confused as he slowly turned and looked up at her.

"What happened to you?" she gasped.

"What are you doing here?" he winced. "You're not supposed to -"

He let out a brief groan, as if trying to move

had caused intense pain somewhere in his battered and broken body.

"I'm getting you to the hospital," she told him.

"No," he whispered.

"You don't have a choice." She turned to go to her backpack. "I'm -"

"No!" he hissed, grabbing her by the wrist and holding her in place. "Didn't you just hear me? No doctors! No hospital! I'm fine, or... I will be."

"You're really hurt," she pointed out.

"I've had worse," he replied, trying to smile before gasping again. "And you should see the other guy. I gave as good as I got."

"Were you in a fight?"

"What's wrong?" he asked, pushing through the pain and forcing himself to sit up, then leaning back against the wall. "Don't I seem like the kind of guy who'd be able to hold his own? Did you have me pegged as some kind of weakling?"

"This is insane," she told him, as she saw cuts on one side of his face and a heavy bruise that seemed to be spreading out from his cheek. "Who did this to you?"

"My -"

He caught himself just in time, but after a few seconds he let out a long sigh.

"Family trouble."

"Someone in your family did this?" she

replied, barely able to believe such a shocking idea. "Michael, is anything broken?"

"I think so," he told her, "but like I said, it's going to be fine." He looked over at the window. "It'll be dark soon. I just need to wait for the moon to change a little more, and then I'll be able to heal completely. Until then, I just need to stay right here and try to conserve energy." He looked up at her, and after a moment he reached toward her face and ran a finger against her skin. "Don't look so worried. I'm sorry I missed our date, I would have done anything to be there but... I just couldn't."

"What happened to you?" she asked again, and now tears were starting to fill her eyes. One of those tears quickly escaped, running down her cheek only for Michael to quickly wipe it away. "Who beat you up?"

"One of my brothers and I had a little disagreement," he explained. "It happens from time to time. Believe it or not, this is how we usually settle things. I know it looks bad, but neither of us backed down so inevitably this happened. I was going to come and see you again, just as soon as I'm better, and ask you for another chance. I know I don't deserve that, and there are probably lots of guys who want to see you, but I was at least going to try."

"What are you talking about?" she asked, before seeing blood drying all over the front of his jacket. "What other injuries have you got, Michael? I need to be sure you're not bleeding to death!"

***

He let out another gasp as cold water ran down his bare back. The skin was cut to ribbons in place, exposing patches of meat; sitting hunched in the metal bathtub in corner of the cabin, Michael shivered slightly as blood trickled into the water and mixed with the dirt and grime.

"I really think you need to see a doctor," Lisa said, as she took the rag and used it to gently add more water to his wounds. "Some of these are really deep."

"You're doing a great job."

"I only know vet stuff."

"That might be more appropriate than you realize."

"What do you mean?"

"I mean that you're doing fine," he replied, half turning to her. He was hugging his own knees close to his face, keeping much of his naked body hidden from view. "You don't need to be doing anything at all."

"At least there's no sign of infection," she said, peering more closely at one of the deeper wounds on his back. "Michael, exactly what happened here? These looks like claw marks."

"They are."

"Did you get attacked by those wolves?"

"Wolf attacks are an occupational hazard in this part of the world."

"But you said your brother -"

"Can we knock it off?" he snapped, momentarily letting his anger through before shaking his head. "Damn it, I should have locked the door. Why did you even come out here, anyway? Are you crazy? You of all people should know that it's not safe in this forest!"

"I brought Dad's rifle."

"That wouldn't necessarily help."

"And I have a support sock kind of thing for my ankle," she continued, "so that didn't hurt too much. I'm a little lucky that I found the path so easily, though. I guess I was just desperate to get here." She wiped some more dried blood from the side of his back, while taking care not to press against any of the larger cuts. "As it happens, I didn't see or hear anything out there. The entire forest seemed pretty much empty all the way here."

"That's not surprising," he told her. "They will have retreated to lick their wounds closer to our own territory. They wouldn't want to be in this part of the forest, not when they're weak."

"You like talking in riddles, don't you?"

"Lisa, I appreciate your help," he replied, "but you really shouldn't be here. It's not safe. But it's going to get dark soon and you shouldn't be out in the forest once the light goes."

"There's no way I'm leaving you here."

"Lisa -"

"So you can just put a sock in it," she added firmly. "If you're staying here tonight, then so am I. I don't care if it's cold. I brought some snacks and I have water too, so we'll be fine. And then tomorrow we're going to talk about what to do with you, because I really think you need to get checked out at the Overflow." She waited for an answer, but after a moment she realized that he was starting to shiver. "How do you live out here?" she muttered, grabbing the towel she'd brought in her backpack and using it to try patting him dry. "*Why* do you live out here? Michael, there's so much you haven't told me and I'm only just starting to try to piece it all together. Aren't you -"

"Stop that!" he said angrily, snatching the towel from her hands and then hesitating for a few seconds. "Can you turn around or wait upstairs or something?" he continued. "I just need to do this myself."

"Fine," she replied, turning and heading to the stairs, "but I'm not leaving you here. One way or another, I'm going to get you to tell me what's really going on."

"No-one's forcing you to stay," he sneered.

"I know that," she snapped. "I'm here

because I care. Believe it or not, I actually want to help you."

She hurried up to the room above, and then she stopped as she heard the sound of Michael slowly standing up in the tin bath. Spotting a small gap in the floorboards, she got down onto her hands and knees and peered through, just in time to see him from behind, standing naked in the tub with river of bloodied water flowing down his body and dribbling into the collection already gathered around his feet. She watched as he tried to dry himself, but she could already tell that he was finding the process far too painful; although she desperately wanted to hurry down and help him, instead she simply turned away from the hole in the floor and looked across the cabin's gloomy attic room.

The sun was starting to set outside, casting long shadows through the window at the top of the far wall. Still able to hear Michael bumping about downstairs, Lisa was starting to realize that she was involved in something that she truly didn't understand. All she knew for certain was that something was clearly very wrong with Michael, and that at some point she had to find some way to help him.

AMY CROSS

CHAPTER ELEVEN

Today...

"I'LL SEND SOMEONE TO relieve you soon," John said as he stepped out of his car and pushed the door shut, before heading toward his front door. "No, Tommy, it's fine. I understand that you've been there for most of the day. There's no way you can stay alert for that long. Maurice or one of the others will be with you by eight."

Once he'd slipped his phone away, he took a set of keys from his pocket.

"That sounded nice," a voice said suddenly, coming from the shadows nearby. "You obviously care a lot about the people who work under you."

Turning, John saw the familiar figure of his son Nick stepping into view.

"Shame you're not so good with family members," Nick continued. "I get it, though. You're a busy man and I should never have expected you to even remember our plans for tonight. I waited an hour at that bar for you to show up, but eventually I realized that this whole trip up north has been a waste of time. Don't worry, though, because I won't bother you again." He turned to walk away. "Goodbye, Dad."

"Nick, wait..."

Stopping, Nick kept his back to his father for a few seconds before slowly turning to him.

"I'm sorry I forgot our arrangement," John said cautiously. "As you might have noticed, with the power off things in Sobolton are pretty difficult at the moment. I've been dealing with a whole host of problems that have been coming at me all day, and I guess I... I just forgot."

"Yeah, I figured that part."

"Why don't we reschedule for tomorrow?" John asked, although he was displaying no real sign of enthusiasm. "I'm sure the power will be back on. We could meet at the same bar, maybe even at the same time. Does that work for you?"

He waited for an answer, but at first Nick seemed lost for words.

"I don't know, Dad," the younger man said finally. "Is there really any point? The last thing I want to do is drag you kicking and screaming to somewhere you don't want to be."

"I never -"

"Because that's how it feels," Nick added, cutting him off. "It's how it's felt for years. I get it, you're the big strong law enforcement guy and I'm the scrappy kid who got into trouble with the law and went to jail. I'm an embarrassment, I'm the exact opposite of what you wanted me to be. And I can't even blame you for being unable to hide that disappointment. Even though I've turned my life around, even though I'm married and I've got a good job, you're never going to be able to get over what I did. And that's fine, we just both need to accept the fact."

"You've arrived at a very difficult time," John told him. "If you'd called ahead -"

"I didn't have your number," Nick spat back. "You didn't even think to let me know you were leaving New York. I only found out because Mom heard from someone else. There was no message, no note, no contact details. You just packed up and moved away, and now here you are trying to start a new life in this pathetic little town. I mean, no offense, but are you completely out of your mind?"

"An opportunity came up and I took it," John explained. "I'm sorry I didn't let you know, but I just hadn't gotten around to that yet."

"And you never would have," Nick replied, "because you just wanted to leave everything in the past. How's the blood pressure these days, by the way? Still on the medication?"

"I'm sorry I missed our meeting," John said, turning and opening the door to his house, then stepping inside and glancing back at his son. "It's late and I need to get on with some paperwork. Drop by the station tomorrow and we can find a time to get a coffee, something like that. There's a nice little diner across the road from where I work, we can go there for lunch."

"I don't even think I'll be around," Nick told him. "I'm only booked at the motel until the morning and right now I see no point extending."

"Well..." John hesitated. "Have a nice drive. And next time let me know if you're coming and I'll try to be more available. Give my regards to your mother. I hope she and Malcolm are doing well." He hesitated again, before gently pushing the door shut.

"You're a really bad dad, Dad," Nick replied, before letting out a sigh as he realized that his father couldn't even hear him. Turning, he sighed again as he wandered over to his car. "I should never have bothered coming up here. This was a huge mistake."

***

Standing at the window in his darkened front room,

John held the drapes aside and watched as his son's car slowly drove around the corner. Once the taillights were out of sight, John let go of the drapes and stepped back, and he stood in silence for a few minutes before allowing himself a big, heavy sigh.

"Probably for the best," he muttered under his breath.

He knew he had to get to work, but in that moment he simply continued to stand in the pitch-black room, replaying the conversation with his son over and over. Some part of him felt that he should perhaps have dealt with the situation better, that he should have been a little more open, but at the same time he reasoned that he was a busy man with a lot of responsibilities; he couldn't be expected to drop everything just because someone arrived unannounced, not when he had a blackout to deal with on top of the Little Miss Dead case and various other problems. No-one in their right mind should just show up in a town and demand to become the center of attention just because a lot of time had passed, no-one in the whole world had a right to try to make themselves more important than the safety and security of a town filled with more than 60,000 souls.

Then again, he knew that his son had always had a heightened sense of his own importance.

Feeling a buzzing sensation in his pocket, he slipped his phone out and saw a familiar name flashing on the screen.

"Bob," he said as he answered, "do you have any news for me?"

"Not the kind you're probably expecting," Robert Law replied as John switched the lights on and headed into the kitchen. "It's more of a bureaucratic thing, really. My favorite. Anyway, turns out there's a strange little law round these parts concerning the burial of unidentified bodies. When you came up with a name for Little Miss Dead, you triggered something."

John opened the fridge and looked inside; his face was bathed in a faint glow as he saw that he had precious little food.

"What exactly did it trigger?" he asked.

"Well, now we have a name for her, we can go ahead and bury her," Robert explained. "Yeah, I know, it's kind of a stupid rule, but I didn't make it. Anyway, we've had her in the chiller for a while now and... I don't know, John, that hasn't been sitting right with me. Obviously it's entirely up to you, but I don't really see that we're going to find her family at any point soon. So do you think..."

His voice trailed off.

"Do I think we should bury the poor girl?" John asked, taking out some cheese slices and a few slices of bread, then bumping the fridge door shut and heading to the other counter. "I'm with you on this one. I hate thinking about her on that cold metal slab. If you really don't think that we need to retain her body for further tests, then I'm minded to think that we should do the right thing."

"At least then she might be able to rest in peace," Robert suggested.

John glanced around the room, worried that he might spot Little Miss Dead – or Eloise, as she seemed to be called – lurking once more in the shadows. There was no sign of her, at least not now, but he still couldn't quite shake the fear that she could show up at any moment. Although he wasn't ready to believe in ghosts just yet, he figured that at the very least his subconscious mind might relax a little if he knew the girl was where she belonged now, which meant putting her six feet under.

"John?"

"Start on the paperwork," John replied. "I'm sure that'll take a while, and then when it finally comes through we can see where we are." He rubbed the back of his neck. "I need to do a few things and then I'm heading back out to the site where the pylon's being repaired. There's been some wolf activity and I need to make sure that the team's safe while they finish up their work."

"Do you ever sleep?"

"Lately, not so much," John admitted.

"Bad dreams?"

"Something like that." He paused, still watching the darkness at the end of the room, still worried that the dead little girl might appear again. "I've got to go, Bob," he added finally. "Keep me in the loop when you hear back about the burial process."

CHAPTER TWELVE

1984...

A WOLF HOWLED IN the distance, far off in the moonlit forest, as Lisa peered out through the cabin's upstairs window. A moment later she heard the howl of a second wolf, as if to answer the first; both wolves seemed to be far away, but she still hated the thought that they were out there at all.

"You're completely safe."

Startled, she spun around and saw that Michael was standing right behind her.

"Sorry," he continued, dressed once again in his black clothes, which were a little torn in places. "I kind of had a feeling that you hadn't heard me coming up."

"I was just... taking a look at the forest," she

admitted. "I couldn't sleep."

"I don't blame you," he replied. "This place hasn't become any more comfortable since your last time here. I'd have tried to make some changes if I'd known you were ever going to be..."

His voice trailed off.

"Well, you know what I mean," he added, clearly a little uncomfortable now. "You really don't have to be here, you know. I'm fine."

"You're not fine," she told him, before squinting a little as she realized that most of the cuts on his face seemed to have healed already. She stepped closer, and sure enough she saw that he already looked a lot better, even if she knew that he couldn't possibly have healed so fast. "The light's not so good," she said finally, figuring that must be the explanation. "Michael, you're not going to get rid of me that easily. You still haven't really told me what happened to you and how you ended up in such a bad state."

"Lisa -"

"Do you think you can keep deflecting?" she asked. "Seriously? Because you can't, and I'm going to keep asking over and over until you tell me the truth. I can help you, Michael, but not unless you're completely honest with me."

"Lisa, please just -"

"Because something's not right here," she said firmly, "and I won't stop digging until I get to the truth. What's really going on, Michael? Why are you living out here in some rundown old cabin? Who beat you up? Why do you act like -"

Before she could get another word out, he leaned forward and kissed her; what had been intended as a simple peck on the lips designed to stop her talking quickly changed, however, and became a passionate kiss that ended with him pressing her against the wall. The kiss continued for a moment longer until Michael pulled back a little, and they stared at one another with matching expressions of surprise.

"I'm sorry," he stammered, "I..."

His voice trailed off.

"Do you seriously think that'll stop me asking questions?" she replied.

"No," he said, shaking his head and stepping back a little further. "Lisa, for your own sake, you need to go home and forget about me. I'll make sure you get there safely, and then you *have* to pretend that none of this happened. You can't look back, you can't tell anyone about me, you have to just get on with your life. No good can ever come of you being involved in this."

"Involved in what?" she asked.

"I can't believe this is happening again," he sighed. "Just stay up here, try to get some sleep and stay warm, and tomorrow first thing I'll take you home. It was just bad luck that you got caught up in this and ended up here again. I won't let that happen for a third time."

He hesitated, and then he turned and made his way toward the top of the wooden staircase.

"What if I *want* to be involved?" she asked.

Stopping, he turned to her again. At that moment another wolf howled somewhere in the distance, far off in the forest.

"What if I want to know everything?" Lisa continued, her voice trembling a little with fear. "What if I want this to happen?"

"You don't," he said firmly. "Believe me, it's just better if you stay out of it. You've almost been killed twice. I won't let that happen again."

***

A short while later, having contemplated exactly what to say, Lisa reached the bottom of the staircase and saw that Michael was standing at the window, staring out at the moonlit forest.

"Deja vu," she said nervously.

He turned to her.

"Another night in your dingy old cabin," she continued, managing half a smile. "You're right, it really hasn't gotten any better. How do you manage not to be cold all the time?"

"I have my ways."

Making her way over to join him, she

looked out at the forest and saw moonlight picking out the tops of the trees. For a few seconds she could only think of the vast inhospitable wilderness that stretched out for miles and miles in every direction; sometimes she felt as if Sobolton was nestled in the biggest clearing of them all, and that the forest was somehow always threatening to push back in and reclaim the land taken by the town. Those thoughts were only encouraged now as she saw the moon hanging high in the night sky.

"When I was a kid," she said cautiously, aware that Michael was looking at her but keeping her gaze fixed on the view outside, "my dad used to take me out and try to teach me to hunt. I never understood why, as a veterinarian, he'd spend his working days trying to help animals and then he'd go out and shoot them."

She paused, struggling to fight the urge to turn and look Michael in the eyes.

"So whenever he tried to get me to shoot," she continued, "I'd always intentionally miss. Sometimes I'd make my hands tremble slightly, just to make it more convincing. Dad always goes on about hunting being a way for a man to reconnect with the natural world, and to be honest I think he might be right. I just personally never wanted to get involved in all of that. I guess I sound pretty stupid, huh?"

"Not at all," Michael said softly. "Not for

one second."

"The thing is," she added, "he really persisted. Like, he took me out a load of times. And even though I always made sure to miss, and to not shoot straight, sometimes I think that everything he taught me still went into my head. Like, despite my best efforts, I still absorbed it all and I could put it into action if necessary. I think I probably could hunt quite well. Hell, sometimes I think I might be a better shot than Dad. Whenever I missed the target, I always knew exactly *how* I was going to miss it."

"Sounds like I'd better make sure I never get in the sights of your rifle," Michael suggested with a faint smile.

"I'm probably completely wrong about all of that," she said, allowing herself a brief, faint smile. "If I actually tried to shoot something, I'd probably miss by a country mile."

"I'm not so sure about that," he replied, watching the side of her face. "I know what it's like to go against your instincts. To go against what people want you to be. I know how it feels to disappoint them, and to pretend you don't care when really deep down you care so much. Sometimes the only way to deal with all of that is to remove yourself so that it's just you against the world. That way, you don't have to worry about what other people think, not unless they keep butting in. Which they might do, from time to time, but you hope that eventually they'll get the message and leave you alone forever. Then maybe you can just try to be who you want to be, and *what* you want to be, without them getting involved."

Now it was his turn to fall silent for a few seconds.

"But then you end up needing them," he added with a sigh, "because they're part of your world and you just can't help but get involved. It's almost like sometimes the universe just forces you to be together, and it won't stop trying to make that happen. You can fight back, but the universe just gets increasingly unsubtle until eventually it gets its way anyway. You have to see the people you've been avoiding, or you have to get involved in their lives." He paused again. "Or you have to wander into their territory and end up asking them questions they refuse to answer."

She turned to him.

"It's late," he muttered, immediately looking across the cabin's gloomy interior. "You should get some sleep."

"It's too cold for that," she pointed out.

"Then I'll keep you warm, like last time," he replied. "Come on. Let me take you upstairs."

CHAPTER THIRTEEN

Today...

"NONE OF THIS MAKES sense," John muttered, sitting at his desk as he peered at another set of printouts, using just the light from a small lamp. "Why would Joe do all of this?"

For the past hour, he'd been going through various records relating to Joe Hicks and the apartment that had once belonged to Lisa Sondnes. All he'd determined so far was that Joe had been determined to keep the apartment exactly as it had been left, to the extent that he hadn't even allowed anyone to clean it up after what had clearly been some kind of struggle; the more he went through the papers, the more John felt sure that Joe had been hiding something, yet he knew that Joe tended to be quite *good* at keeping things under wraps. In this case, however, the entire process seemed to have been conducted in a very haphazard manner.

Almost panicked.

Turning to another page, he saw what appeared to be a letter from a place called Lakehurst, which was apparently some kind of psychiatric hospital far away. The letter concerned Lisa Sondnes, who had apparently been a patient there for a short period, but there was no real detail about her time at the institution. The letter had been signed by a Doctor Arthur Campbell, who claimed to have been consulting with various colleagues, but John still couldn't make sense of the whole situation.

Hearing a shuffling sound, he looked across the darkened room. He saw no sign of movement, however, so he quickly forced himself to return his attention to the paperwork.

"The patient shows signs of good progress," he read out loud, "and I'm comfortable with her returning home, although I must stress that she requires strict observation. I'm happy for this to be carried out by her family, who need to know that they can contact my office at any time if they have concerns. If I'm unavailable, one of my colleagues will be more than happy to help."

Hearing the same sound again, he glanced up. There was still nobody else in the room, but

John knew that he might easily trick himself into believing otherwise. Looking back down, he read some more from the page.

"The situation is greatly improved," he continued, "and I'm confident that there will be little to no recurrence of the patient's earlier problems. That being said, I'm mindful of the fact that she's returning to the area where her difficulties manifested, and this obviously raises certain concerns. Her fixation on this Michael individual seems to have faded but it could easily come back if she's reminded of -"

Hearing yet another shuffling sound, John looked up. This time he wasn't even expecting to see anything, but he froze as he saw the dead little girl standing on the other side of the desk, glaring at him with two dead eyes. And then, before John could react, the girl screamed and John pulled back, opening his eyes and jerking up in the chair as he realized that he'd been asleep.

For a moment he simply sat completely still. He stared at the spot where the girl had been standing in his dream, and then he looked down and saw the same paperwork from earlier about Lisa and Lakehurst. He'd been reading those papers when, he realized now, he must have drifted off. And then, feeling a buzzing sensation, he took his phone from his pocket and saw someone from the office was trying to get through.

"Hey," he said, getting to his feet as he answered, "tell the people out at the pylon that I'm on my way. I've been slightly delayed, but I'll be there."

"Sir, it's not that," Carolyn replied, sounding a little troubled about something. "I thought you'd want to know that we just got a call from McGinty's. It seems someone decided to break in after they closed tonight. They smashed the place up and stole the takings from the back room."

***

"I know," Al Burnham muttered, standing in the bar and looking around at all the damage, "it's my fault, I can't blame anyone else. I finally hooked a generator up so I could serve cold beer, but I didn't realize that the alarm system wasn't hooked into the set-up. Clearly someone figured that out, though, because they must've broken through that window less than an hour after I locked the door."

"How much money do you think was taken?" John asked, looking around and seeing broken glass on the floor in front of the window.

"A few hundred," Al admitted. "Business hasn't been great with the power off, but that's still profit that I was counting on. I should've put it in the safe, but I couldn't open it because it's on the same system as the alarms. Damn it, this whole situation's a complete mess. I just feel so stupid, like someone's been watching me screw everything up and then they pounced as soon as the moment was right. That's some pretty scary level of precision, if you ask me."

"Did you have any suspicious people hanging around while you were open?" John asked.

"Just a few of the regulars. Oh, and there was a fella I didn't recognize. Sort of youngish, but not too young. He was sat over there in the corner booth, just kinda keeping himself to himself. He didn't say much. In fact, I got the impression that he was pretty annoyed about something toward the end. I think maybe he'd been waiting for someone who just didn't show up."

"Is that so?" John replied, immediately thinking back to his conversation with Nick earlier in the night.

Turning, he looked over at the bar, and already his mind was racing. There were already a lot of similarities between this particular break-in and one he'd dealt with a while back in New York; in fact, the more he surveyed the scene, the more he realized that the similarities were only mounting, to the extent that he began to feel a growing sense of dread in the pit of his stomach. No matter how hard he tried to tell himself that he was imagining connections that couldn't possibly be real, his mind was racing as he began to feel a little nauseous.

"What about liquor?" he asked finally.

"What about it?"

"Is any liquor missing?" he continued.

"I haven't really had a chance to check. Everything looks kinda okay on the shelves."

"What about your most expensive bottle?"

"That'll be one of the old whiskeys I keep under the counter," Al said, heading around the bar to take a look. "Most people don't even know about it, I keep it for special occasions but -"

Stopping suddenly, he leaned down and took a look at one of the shelves. When he stood up, he seemed troubled by something.

"It's gone," he stammered. "That bottle's worth three hundred dollars! How would someone even know to look for it?" He sighed. "It'd have to be someone who really knows his stuff. I'm talking someone who researching liquor, something like that. I'm not even sure there are many people in Sobolton who'd have a clue about the damn stuff. Hey, do you think this was all done by an outsider? What if some opportunist from out of town happened to pass through, and he figured that with the power off he had a chance to break in? He took the money from the back room, and then he had a look around and spotted that bottle. Is that at all possible?"

"I don't see why not," John said through gritted teeth. "After all, it wouldn't be the first time."

"Now..."

Al paused, furrowing his brow as if he was trying to figure something out.

"I don't want to sound paranoid," he continued cautiously, "but do you remember how I mentioned there was a guy in earlier I didn't recognize?"

"I do," John said darkly.

"I feel bad for suggesting this," Al added, "but you don't think that guy could have been casing the place, do you? I mean, he seemed more annoyed than anything, he kept watching the door like he expected someone to come through. I tried to make small-talk with him, just to see how he was doing, but he shut me down pretty fast. He asked a few questions about you, though. Hey, Sheriff Tench, the more I think about it, the more I feel like the guy really seemed to be on the lookout. Damn it, I wish the cameras were working, so I could show you a picture of him."

"That's okay, Al," John said, taking a deep breath as he felt a sense of utter dread and fury spreading through his chest. "I know exactly where to find him."

CHAPTER FOURTEEN

1984...

"THEY SOUND CLOSER," LISA whispered, on the floor upstairs in the cabin as Michael kept his arms around her. "Are they closer, or am I imagining it?"

They lay in silence for a moment, waiting in case another wolf howled somewhere.

"Slightly," Michael admitted finally, "but you really don't need to worry about it, because you're -"

"Because I'm safe here," she said, cutting him off with a faint smile. "Yeah, you keep saying that and I guess I have no reason to doubt you." She paused, relieved that she could hear only silence now. "I swear I grew up being told that there weren't wolves around here."

"You did?"

"Is that wrong?" She paused, before shuffling around onto her back so that she could see his face in the moonlight. "I mean, it's definitely wrong, isn't it?" she added. "There are clearly wolves."

He nodded.

"So why do people always say that there aren't?" she asked.

"You've got me on that one," he replied. "Then again, people say the craziest things sometimes. I guess if the people of Sobolton want to kind of... collectively deny reality, then it's nobody else's place to stop them." He paused, looking down into her eyes. "But there have been wolves around here for a really long time," he continued. "There have been wolves here for a lot longer than there have been people. There were even wolves here before Sobolton existed."

"Is that right?"

"This was all wolf territory," he explained, "as far as the eye could see, from horizon to horizon in every direction. Then when people came, I guess the wolves accepted that part of their land was going to be taken. They probably didn't even mind a small human settlement, since they'd be able to scavenge from time to time. But then that small settlement became a little bigger, then it became bigger still, and then it just kept growing and taking more and more of the land that the wolves called their own. And that's not all, because suddenly parts of the forest were getting ripped down so that those big pylons could be installed, and then those powerlines were run through the place and..."

His voice trailed off, as if he felt that he'd perhaps said too much.

"I'm just guessing, of course," he said, somewhat unconvincingly. "There's a lot of... stuff out here."

"Stuff?"

"Two worlds," he continued. "That's all you've got to remember. There are two worlds, and that means there are three territories."

"Three?" She furrowed her brow. "How does that work? If there are two worlds, then -"

"There's their world," he added, cutting her off, "and there's our world, and then the third world is the kind of overlap between the two. I think the word for it is the ecotone, where the two worlds transition between one and the other. Of course, that only works if both sides respect the ecotone and aren't continually pushing to move it further and further back. That's why we... I mean, why some of us..."

He paused again.

"I didn't agree with the idea of creating that gate," he told her. "Especially not the way they went about it. When the wind blows through those bones, I get a chill every time."

"I have absolutely no idea what you're talking about," she replied, still staring up at him.

"Exactly," he said firmly, "and we should keep it that way. Like it or not, the ecotone has to be maintained, it's a kind of no man's land and that's really important. It might be more important than anyone on either side realizes."

"You know," she said cautiously, "sometimes I feel like you're just talking in riddles, but other times I feel as if you know a hell of a lot more than you're even letting on. It's as if you're hinting at something so much bigger."

"I'm talking too much," he told her. "You really need to get some sleep. Are you warm yet?"

"Surprisingly, I am," she replied, turning and looking over at the window.

For the next few minutes, they lay in place, with Michael still holding Lisa in his arms. They were both listening to the silence outside, waiting for the next wolf howl, although the silence persisted and eventually Lisa began to feel as if Michael's promises of safety were real. She began to pay more attention to the sound of his breath, and to the tiny shifts in his arms as he continued to hold her; soon she noticed even smaller details, and she began to become aware not only of her own beating heart but his as well. The silence was becoming so much stronger now, and Lisa was starting to feel as if neither of them ever needed to speak again. Yet in the end, she was the one who spoke first, after slowly rolling onto her back once more and looking up at him.

"Hey," she softly finally, "maybe you need to stop me talking again."

"You're not talking," he pointed out.

"I know," she replied, before leaning closer and kissing him gently on the lips. She pulled back slightly, watched his eyes to study his reaction, and then she kissed him again.

***

Morning sunlight streamed through the window as Lisa opened her eyes. Blinking, she immediately felt as if something was very different, as if her own body had changed somehow. She turned and looked over her bare shoulder, and she saw that Michael was sleeping naked next to her.

Sitting up, she began to run through the events of the previous night. Everything came back to her in brief, frantic snatches: she remembered the sensation of his touch, and the heat of his breath on the side of her neck, and the mingling sweat; she also remembered the way they'd moved as one, and the sound of her own voice whispering into his ear. All these fragments of memory seemed so chaotic, yet somehow they began to settle and she felt a warm shiver pass through her body as she realized that there was no going back now. 'It' had finally happened, and there was no going back to the days when she hadn't known how it felt to finally be with someone.

Creeping out from under the shabby old blanket, taking care to not disturb Michael, she began to quietly gather her clothes. She slipped them back on and got to her feet, and then she headed to the window and looked out at the bright morning. She knew she was probably imagining things to a certain extent, but she couldn't shake the feeling that her entire body was so very different now, that she'd emerged from her old form like a butterfly that had finally unfolded itself from its chrysalis.

Something moved outside, in the shadows of the treeline.

"You look so beautiful," Michael said suddenly, "and the craziest part is that you don't even realize it, do you?"

Turning, she saw that he was watching her.

"Hey," she said, suddenly feeling very shy and more than a little embarrassed. "Sorry, I didn't mean to wake you up."

"I was awake already," he explained. "I was just... enjoying being here with you."

"Yeah," she replied, "me too."

"Come over here," he replied, gesturing for her to join him. "Hey, Lisa, while we still have time. You know I'd wait forever for you, right?"

"You'd..."

She paused, wondering just why he'd phrased things like that. Part of her just wanted to crawl away and hide, and try to make sense of everything, but she knew that wasn't an option. For perhaps the first time in her life, she needed to be brave.

"I'm sorry," he continued, "that came out wrong. What I meant is that I'm here for you. I'm going to have to get you back to town soon, but I don't want that to be the end of it. Not now. I might regret this, but I want to see you again."

"You might regret it?"

"I'm terrible with words," he said with a grin. "At least, I'm terrible when I'm talking about anything important like this. Let's start again." He took a long, deep breath. "We've got a few hours until I have to get you home, right? Do you want to spend some time together? I feel like, after everything that's happened, we should know each other a little better. But I understand if you'd rather not, I know you've probably got lots of things you need to be doing. If you prefer, I can walk you back to town and we don't ever have to see each other again."

"Of course not," she replied, making her

way back over and kneeling next to him, before tucking a stray strand of hair behind one ear. "Are you crazy? The last thing I'd ever want to do is get out of here, especially after everything that happened last night. I guess... I just need time to process it, you know?"

"Totally," he said, reaching over and taking hold of her hand, then giving it a gentle squeeze. "We've got all the time in the world."

CHAPTER FIFTEEN

Today...

"SO HE DIDN'T MENTION anything about that at all?" Tommy asked, still sitting in his cruiser across from Lisa's old apartment. "He didn't say anything about sending someone to take my place?"

"You have no idea how busy things have been around here this evening," Carolyn replied over the phone, her voice positively dripping with frustration. "I swear this blackout has been bringing the worst out of people. At least the landline's down, which helps, but they just keep wandering in with their problems."

"Okay," Tommy said cautiously, before pausing for a moment to think. "I'm not complaining, so please don't make Sheriff Tench think that I am, it's just that I've been here for a lot of hours now and I was kind of thinking I might like to get home and see Tracy and Josh, that's all. I like to get home before they go to bed, and I'm on shift tomorrow so it's not like I'll get much time to sleep as it is."

He paused, still watching the building on the other side of the street.

"But I know Sheriff Tench is busy, and I'm sure he's going to send someone to relieve me as soon as he gets the chance."

"I'll give him a nudge when he comes back," Carolyn replied. "I think he's off dealing with something at McGinty's, but the second he walks through this door I'll remind him that he's supposed to get someone over to you. How does that sound?"

"It sounds great, thank you," Tommy said. "Sorry to bother you, though. It's really not that important. I can stick it out."

"Someone's coming," she sighed. "I've got to go, Tommy. If this is another local idiot asking when the power's coming back on, I think I'm actually gonna scream."

Smiling as the call cut out, Tommy set the phone back in his pocket and then leaned back in his seat. He could feel the tiredness creeping through his body and threatening to fully take over, but so far he'd been managing to fight the urge to take a nap. He knew that Sheriff Tench wanted him to keep an eye on the old Lisa Sondnes apartment, and even if he didn't quite understand why this was suddenly so important again after so many years, he told himself that he was absolutely going to do his duty without slacking at all.

And then, as he looked across the street again, he spotted a shadow moving down the side of the building.

For a moment, not really knowing what to do, Tommy could only watch the spot where he'd seen the shadow. There was no sign of anything now, but after a few seconds he opened the door of his cruiser and stepped out; he checked that he had his gun, and then he pushed the cruiser's door shut and began to make his way across the street. Looking both ways, he saw no sign of anyone else, but as he approached the front of the small apartment building he couldn't help but wonder why someone might have been sneaking around.

"Probably nothing," he muttered under his breath, trying to make himself feel a little better. "I'm sure it's..."

He swallowed hard as he looked at the narrow alleyway that ran down the side of the building. Making his way over, he found himself staring into darkness; the complete lack of lights down the alley meant that he couldn't see a thing, although after a few seconds he noticed that he'd already began to reach instinctively for his gun. He managed to force himself to stand firm, but the more he stared in the darkness the more he began to feel as if something in that darkness was staring back at him.

"Hello?" he said finally, immediately horrified to hear the unprofessional fear in his voice. He took a moment to steady his nerves. "This is the Sobolton Sheriff's Department," he continued, sounding a little more authoritative this time. "Is there's anyone there, can you please come out and identify yourself? That's... that's an order."

He waited, and after a moment he remembered the flashlight hanging from his belt. Reaching down, he fumbled for a moment before holding the flashlight up, and then he fumbled again as he tried to find the switch on the side. Finally he turned the light on, only to almost blind himself as the beam hit his own eyes. Startled, he swung the beam away, but for a few seconds he could only blink wildly as he tried to clear his vision. He muttered a few curses under his breath, and then finally – once his sight was back to normal – he aimed the flashlight along the alley just to prove to himself that there was no cause for concern.

Almost immediately, he saw a figure standing about halfway along the alley with its back to him.

"Uh, hello?" Tommy called out, holding the flashlight in one hand while reaching down for his gun with the other. "My name is Tommy... I mean, Thomas Marshall, and I'm with the Sobolton Sheriff's Department. Do you mind telling me what you're doing here?"

The figure offered no response, and merely stood with its back still turned to Tommy. This time, Tommy realized that the flashlight's beam was picking out the back of a bare, hairless head, and that the skin on that head appeared to be marked by lots of red patches and strange red lines, almost as if the skin itself was threatening to split apart.

"Uh, Sir?" Tommy continued, almost taking his gun out but forcing himself to leave it for now, keen to avoid escalating what might yet turn out to be a perfectly benign situation. "I don't know if you can hear me? Sir, can you let me know if you can hear me?"

Again he waited, but the figure seemed almost oblivious. After a few seconds Tommy realized that it was standing right next to a window that looked into Lisa's apartment, and he couldn't help but think that somehow that had to be relevant.

"Okay, Sir," he added, determined to take better control of the situation, "I'm going to have to ask you to turn around, alright? I only want to ask you some questions, but you *need* to turn around and face me. Have I made that clear?"

Yet again the figure offered no response. Tommy looked back over at the cruiser and wondered whether he should call for backup, but deep down he figured that everyone at the station would only make fun of him for panicking. The last thing he wanted was for Sheriff Tench to think that he couldn't be trusted with a simple task, so instead he turned and saw that the strange figure still hadn't moved a muscle.

"Okay," he said again, taking his gun out and starting to cautiously make his way along the alley. "I'm approaching you from behind, Sir. I'm sure you absolutely don't want any trouble here, so how about we just have a little chat and then you can tell me what you're up to? Does that sound good?"

The closer he got to the figure, the clearer he saw how dry and damaged the back of its head seemed. The skin was peeling in places, with delicate-looking plates of skin having lifted to reveal sore red patches beneath. As the flashlight's beam picked out the mottled flesh, Tommy even saw a few of those skin flakes falling away and dropping to the ground, as if the man was constantly shedding.

Finally, stopping a few steps away from the man, Tommy realized that something about this entire situation felt decidedly unsettling.

Suddenly he heard his phone ringing in his pocket. As the ringtone played loudly, he reaching down and tried to switch it to silent; when that failed, he had to pull the phone out and take a moment to reject the call, which he saw was coming from his wife. Making a mental note to call her back, he managed to silence the phone after a few seconds, and then he slid it away before looking at the strange figure again. This time, to his shock, he saw that the figure had turned around as if stirred by the phone's sound.

"Okay, that's better," Tommy stammered, shocked by the sight of the alternating bloodied and dried patches that covered the figure's features, as if the man's entire body was starting to flake apart. "Um, I mean... uh, Sir, I don't know if you heard me before but my name is... uh, Tommy... I mean, Thomas Marshall, and I'm with the Sobolton Sheriff's Department, and I saw you out here tonight and I just have to ask you a few questions, okay?"

He waited in silence, but now the man was simply staring back at him with two dark eyes that were swimming with blood in their corners.

"Sir," Tommy continued, "if you don't respond, I -"

In that moment his phone began to ring again. He looked down, but before he could do anything else the figure snarled and lunged at him, slamming him against the wall on one side of the alley before throwing him across to the other side. Crying out, Tommy tried to raise his gun, only for the figure to rip it from his hand. Reaching up, the figure immediately started to press his thumbs against Tommy's eyes, pushing harder and harder until finally he brought and agonized scream from his victim's throat.

CHAPTER SIXTEEN

1984...

SETTING THE PAPERBACK BOOK down, Lisa looked at the cover for a moment and saw the muscle-covered man holding the heroine in her arms. There was something strangely lurid and over-the-top about the image, and she couldn't help but smile as she got to her feet and checked her watch.

"Lisa?" her father called through from the hallway, having just returned from the shops. "Honey? I'm thinking of making a big lunch. How does egg and salmon strike you?"

"It sounds great, Dad," she said, making her way through and grabbing her jacket from the hook, "but -"

"But you're going out again," he sighed. "I should have known. I swear, Lisa, you're barely home at all these days."

He watched as she slipped her feet into her sneakers.

"So when are you gonna admit it?" he asked.

"Admit what?"

"That you're seeing some guy."

She turned to him.

"It's okay," he added with a grin, holding his hands up in mock surrender. "Do I seem horrified? I'm actually quite relieved. But you *could* let me know what's going on, you know. I know I'm your embarrassing, old-fashioned father and you probably hate the idea of introducing me to this guy, but I'd just like to be sure that everything's fine."

"Of course everything's fine," she said, stepping over and kissing him on the cheek.

"What's his name?"

"Dad..."

"At least tell me his name."

She hesitated for a moment.

"Michael."

"Michael?" He chuckled. "Let me think, do I know any Michaels? I know a few. What's his surname?"

"You wouldn't know him," she replied, as she realized that even *she* didn't know Michael's surname. "He's not exactly local. But Dad, I'll introduce you to him eventually, we're just taking things a little slow for now. We're getting to know each other."

"I remember when I was first dating our mother," he told her. "I used to try to think of all these crazy exciting things for us to do, so that she wouldn't think I was boring."

"I've got to go," she replied, checking her watch yet again before stepping away from him and opening the front door, "I have to meet Michael."

"And I wouldn't dream of delaying you," he replied. "Just enjoy yourself, okay? Young love is a great thing, and -"

"Thanks, Dad!"

With that she shut the door, leaving Rod to stand all alone listening to the sound of her footsteps hurrying away from the house.

"Huh," he said, clearly amused by her eagerness. "Kids, huh? Well, I guess I finally got what I wanted all this time. She has a life now." He carried his bag of groceries through to the kitchen and began to take out the eggs and salmon. "More lunch for me. Damn it, at this rate I'm gonna start getting fat!"

He reached over and flicked a switch on the wall, only for the light above the stove to remain off.

"Damn it," he sighed. "Another power

outage? Must be the third one this year already. When are they gonna fix the damn grid properly?"

***

"So Dad's been digging and digging," Lisa said around an hour later, as she and Michael made their way along a path that ran adjacent to the river, way out beyond the edge of town. "Finally I kind of told him about you. Not much, just your name and the fact that you exist."

"What did he say?" Michael asked, sounding a little concerned.

"I think he's just relieved that I'm getting out of the house," she admitted. "He was always nagging me to do more with my time than just read and study. I think maybe it's gone a little too far in the other direction now, but I'm still keeping up with all my studies. After I finished school I took a few years out to help Dad, but now I'm really ready to get back into it all. I'll be slightly older than the other students but I don't mind that. Oh, but I won't have to go far away, so you don't need to worry about that."

Realizing that he hadn't said anything for almost a full minute, she stopped and turned to him.

"Michael? Even if I go away to school, we'll be fine. The last couple of months have been the happiest of my life and there's no way I'd ever let anything come between us." She paused, before stepping back over to him. "But I don't have to do any of that," she added. "I can just stay in Sobolton."

"There's a whole world out there for you to explore," he pointed out. "Don't you want to go and see it?"

"Of course," she replied, "but I don't have to go alone. You could come with me."

She waited for a response, but she could already see from the look in his eyes that he doubted her suggestion. After a moment longer, she steppe back over to him.

"Why are you so tied to this forest?" she asked. "It's as if you can't really leave it, at least not for long."

"Of course I can leave it," he said, although he still seemed a little evasive.

"But you don't," she continued. "Michael, every time I try to ask about your past, and about your family, you find some way to change the subject. I've been patient about that and I've tried not to push you, but I'm starting to worry that in some way you're holding yourself back." She watched his eyes, hoping to see some kind of change but instead recognizing only a hint of fear. "Michael, why do you live in a rickety old wooden cabin in the middle of nowhere, with no power and no real furniture? And why do you live there alone?"

"Lisa -"

"Your usual attempt to deflect won't work this time," she added, before he could get another word out. "Did something happen to you?"

"I just chose this path," he said cautiously. "I didn't want to pick one world or the other, so I'm trying to exist in both. It's not easy, and my family's very much against it, but they've learned to leave me alone. At least for now."

"So what are the two worlds?"

He opened his mouth to reply, before hesitating for a moment.

"Do you feel like you can't tell me?" she asked.

"It's not that."

"Do you feel like I won't understand?"

"Lisa -"

"Or that I'll judge you in some way?"

"It's none of those things," he admitted finally. "It's more that... Lisa, there are some things that are so far beyond your comprehension, and that's a good thing. You don't need to know what's really out here in the forest, you'd only be in danger if you ever found out. That's not just from my side, either. There are people from Sobolton – not a lot, but a few – who are just as keen to make sure that the world's don't cross." He sighed. "I've already let this go to far," he added nervously. "I hate to admit this, but I think we should just cut if off now, before you get too deep into something you can't control."

"I'm sick of being treated like an idiot," she replied. "My dad does it all the time, he thinks I'm some naive little thing who doesn't understand the world. Please don't treat me the same way."

"I'm just scared of drawing you into this," he said, noticeably glancing around as if he worried that they might be spotted at any moment. "I don't know that I can keep you safe forever."

"I don't need you to keep me safe," she told him. "I can look after myself. At least, I can look after myself if you tell me properly what we're dealing with. Or we could just leave together. We could go away to somewhere you'd never be found. If you're really that worried about your family, then why stick around?"

"Everything you're suggesting is completely right," he replied. "I'll tell you more, I promise, just... not yet. When I'm with you, I feel as if that whole world is so far away. I don't want to even think about it right now. The time will come, I'm sure of that, but until then... I want to pretend that none of that is real. Can we do that, Lisa? Can we just be *us* for now? The rest of the world will be along later, but in this moment let's just be us."

"You're very good at talking in riddles," she said, stepping closer and putting her hands on his shoulders. "Just promise me that when the time's right, you'll let me in. Because I don't need to be protected."

"When the time comes, I'll tell you everything," he said firmly, briefly glancing at the trees again before looking back into her eyes. "I swear. On that, you have my word."

CHAPTER SEVENTEEN

Today...

"HANG ON, I'M COMING!" Nick Tench called out, hauling himself off the bed in his dark motel room and stumbling toward the door as someone continued to pound on the other side. "Can you just stop knocking for a moment? I heard you already!"

Barely awake, he pulled the door open and saw two officers from the sheriff's department standing outside.

"What's wrong?" he asked cautiously. "My car's parked fine and -"

"Nicholas Tench?" one of the officers asked.

"Why do you want to know?"

"Mr. Tench, I need you to accompany us to the station," the officer said firmly.

"Right now?"

"Right now."

"It's pretty late," Nick pointed out. "Can you tell me what this is all about? My father -"

"Mr. Tench, are you going to come with us," the officer asked, interrupting him, "or do we have to do this the hard way?"

"I haven't done anything wrong," Nick told him, looking him up and down for a moment before starting to swing the door shut. "Go to Hell," he added, "you can come back tomorrow at a more civilized -"

Before he could finish, the first officer pushed the door open and grabbed Nick, slamming him against the wall while his colleague attached a pair of handcuffs.

"What the hell's wrong with you?" Nick gasped, clearly in pain as he tried in vain to pull away. "I haven't done anything! You can't just come storming in here like this and treat me like I'm some kind of common criminal!"

***

"Keep me informed," John said, standing at his desk in the office. "I'll be out there just as soon as I can, but a few things have come up in town first. It's good that there's been no further sign of the wolves, though. Hopefully that means we'll get the power back on in the next few hours."

"Sir?"

Hearing a knock at the door, he turned and saw Carolyn standing in the doorway.

"You wanted me to let you know when the suspect was ready," she said cautiously. "He's about to be taken into room one, but the guys have a question. It's about the candles, they're really not sure about the safety aspect of questioning someone by candlelight if the generators fail. We've looked through all the manuals and there's nothing mentioned about what to do if we don't have power."

"Leave that to me," John said firmly. "I'm on my way."

Once he'd cut the call, and with Carolyn having headed back along the corridor, John stood alone for a moment with a single electric light buzzing gently above him. Pretty much an entire twenty-four hours had now elapsed since the power had gone out, and any sense of novelty had long worn off; there had been a couple of teasing hints that things might pick up, brief moments when the power had returned but only for a second or two. Now that he faced a possible second night of trying to keep order in Sobolton during a blackout, John couldn't help but worry that even the station's generator might eventually fail, at which point chaos might break out entirely.

He turned and headed to the door, taking a moment to switch the light off, and then – with his back to the darkened room – he froze as he heard the distinctive sound of his office chair creaking under someone's weight.

Slowly, he looked over at the desk and saw that the empty chair was exactly where it had been left, with no sign of anyone. Still, even in his relatively short time in Sobolton he'd come to recognize the sound that chair made whenever anyone sat down, and he knew such a sound couldn't simply occur spontaneously.

"Hello?" he said cautiously, worried that the dead little girl might be about to make another appearance.

He waited, but deep down he already felt that this wasn't her style. The girl tended to appear more directly, and she'd certainly never made use of the furniture before. John continued to watch the empty office chair, and after a few seconds he noticed that the room seemed to have become markedly colder. Finally, determined to prove to himself that nothing was wrong, he kept the lights off as he made his way over, and he spun the chair around so that he was facing the empty spot.

Reaching down, he moved his hands through the air, but he felt absolutely nothing. He looked around the office, and he still couldn't help but notice that the room remained unusually cold.

"Are you here?" he asked. "Your name's Eloise, isn't it? I don't know your surname yet, but at least your first name's a start. I know the progress might not be as rapid as you'd like, but we're getting there. We'll find the answers eventually. On that, you have my word."

Still staring at the empty chair, he realized that most likely he was talking to thin air. He waited for a moment longer, and then he turned and left the room, walking along the corridor until he reached the reception area and then heading toward the interrogation rooms.

"Oh, Sir?" Carolyn called over to him.

He stopped and turned to look at her.

"I almost forgot," she continued, "Tommy called a while back."

"Damn it, I'm supposed to get someone to relieve him," he replied.

"He mentioned that. He didn't sound annoyed or anything, but you know what Tommy's like, he's not exactly the kind of guy who wants to cause trouble. He just said that he'd be grateful if you could get someone out there to take over for him."

"I'll do that just as soon as I'm done with the suspect."

"If you like, I could find a -"

"No, I'll do it," he said, cutting her off. "Sorry, I didn't mean to be short with you. Before I send someone out there to watch of the apartment, I need to brief them myself so they know what to look out for. I'll sort it out, I promise."

"Sure," she replied, forcing a smile. "I'm going to head home soon, but I'll be back in the morning. Hopefully by then we'll have some juice."

"That'd be nice," he muttered, turning and heading along the next corridor, taking out his phone in the process and quickly bringing up Tommy's number.

Stopping at the door to the first interrogation room, he tapped to call. While he waited for Tommy to answer, he couldn't help but feel that he was being pulled in too many different directions all at once. The situation out at the pylon seemed to have settled for now, but he knew he had to get over there and take charge in case the wolves returned; at the same time, he also knew that he needed to push on with the Little Miss Dead investigation and try to figure out how the name Eloise might allow him to figure things out further, but on top of that people were asking more and more questions about Joe's death and he also had to contend with lingering questions about the Lisa Sondnes case. And on top of all of that, he still hadn't quite managed to get his head around everything that had happened during his encounter with the supposed ghost of Amanda Mathis, which didn't make much sense.

And then...

Swallowing hard, he looked at the door to the interrogation room. He could feel a sense of dread pulling at his chest, and he told himself that this was one case that he could easily turn over to one of the other officers. At the same time, he felt absolutely certain that he had a duty to deal with this situation himself.

"This is Tommy Marshall," the voice on the phone suddenly said. "I can't answer right now, but if you leave a message, I'll get back to you real soon."

"Tommy, this is John Tench," he replied. "I'm sorry I haven't sent anyone out to take over from you, but I'm going to get that sorted within the next hour. Just hang on tight and... I'm sorry you've been there for so long. I appreciate your time, though. Call me back when you get this."

After cutting the call, he hesitated again, still very much wishing that he didn't have to deal with the next problem. At the same time, he prided himself on facing reality, so finally he pushed the door open and stepped into the room, and he forced himself to make eye contact with the suspect sitting at the table.

"Alright, Hodges," he told the deputy, "you can leave us."

"Sir, what about -"

"I'm going to do this alone," John said firmly. "I know that's not strictly in line with protocol, but just trust me on this, okay?"

"Whatever you say," Hodges replied, heading out into the corridor and then pulling the door shut.

Walking over to the table, John looked down at the suspect who remained seated on the other side.

"Hey, Dad," Nick said, staring back up at him. "You know, when I said we should talk, this wasn't exactly what I had in mind."

***

Back in John's darkened office, the chair next to the desk was slowly turning. After a few seconds it stopped, as if lost in thought, before letting out a faint creaking sound as it began to turn the other way.

CHAPTER EIGHTEEN

1984...

"HEY," MICHAEL SAID SLEEPILY, having just stirred from a deep sleep. "What are you looking at?"

"Hmm?"

Standing at the window of the cabin, looking out at the trees, Lisa realized for a moment that she wasn't quite sure how to answer that question. The sun was setting outside on another day, and she already knew that she wanted to stay at the cabin for the night rather than making the long walk back into town.

"I don't actually know, to be honest," she admitted. "Habit, I guess."

Spotting one of the candles she'd brought

from home, she set about lighting it with a match. Once that was done, she set it carefully in her mother's old candle-holder and placed it on the sill.

"Come over here," Michael said. "Hey, Lisa, while we still have time. You know I'd wait forever for you, right?"

"And where exactly do you think I'd be?" she asked, smiling as she turned to him. "I'm not going anywhere."

"You shouldn't let yourself get tied down."

"I'm not," she insisted. "I don't *have* to leave Sobolton. I don't have to study veterinary sciences, not if I don't want to. I can just stay here and -"

"I love you," he said suddenly, interrupting her. "There, I said it. You don't have to say it back, not if you don't want to. I won't be offended. I just thought you should know that I'll always be here for you. I know things are difficult but I'll wait. And I'll always look after you."

"I..."

Her voice trailed off for a moment.

"I know I'm moving fast," Michael continued, "but that's only because I know how quickly things can change. If anything bad happened, I'd want you to know how I really feel."

"I love you too," she replied, feeling tears welling in her eyes. "Damn it, this is like one of those stupid books I read so much, but... I just know it deep down, in my heart. So why not admit it?"

"I know there are things about me that you hate," he told her. "The secrets, for one, and the fact that I can't tell you everything for another. I can't change all of them, but I'll do my best. My love for you is complete and unconditional. Now that you've lit the candle, why don't you come over and sit with me for a while?"

Unable to resist the temptation, she made her way over, with a blanket still wrapped around her bare body. She'd brought as many items from home as she could carry, hoping to make the cabin just a little nicer, and as she knelt next to Michael she found herself wondering just how much more she could do to fix the place up. Looking around, she saw a few books and bags of snacks, and she couldn't shake the sense that everything seemed so temporary, as if the cabin might never feel like a proper home. Her father's spare rifle was resting in the corner, leaning against the wall.

Turning to Michael again, she saw that he was staring up at her.

"What?" she asked.

"What?" he replied.

"I said it first."

"I was just thinking about how open you are," he explained. "I've always felt that there are things I can't tell anyone, but with you it's different. Lisa, I think..."

He hesitated.

"What do you think?" she asked, feeling a growing sense of anticipation in her chest. "You can tell me anything, Michael. You have to know that."

He opened his mouth to reply, but for a few seconds he held back before turning and grabbing his clothes.

"I want to make a fire," he said, clearly hoping to delay things for a little while longer. "We can sit outside and talk, and at least we'll be warm."

"Michael, what were you about to -"

"Wait here," he added, already slipping into his shirt as he turned and looked down at her. "I don't want us to have another night shivering in the cold. This time we're going to be warm. And then I'll tell you everything. The good parts, the bad parts, all of it. I won't leave anything out, and Lisa..." He paused again, clearly worried about what might happen next. "You deserve the full truth," he continued finally. "Tonight you're going to get every last word of it."

***

Flames were spitting and crackling as the fire continued to burn, on a patch of ground just a short way from the steps at the front of the cabin. Wearing one of Michael's old shirts, which covered her almost down to her knees, Lisa stepped into the doorway and looked out just in time to see him adding some more logs to the fire.

"How's it going?" she asked.

"Almost there," he replied, smiling at her with a hint of nervousness as light from the flames danced on one side of his face. "I just need another half hour or so."

"This is almost starting to look slightly romantic," she told him. "I've got to say, I'm impressed."

Turning and heading back inside, she wandered over to her backpack and pulled it open. She took out a couple of cans of beer, which she'd been saving for the right moment; she'd never really been much of a drinker, preferring to avoid ending up like her father, but she figured that for once she could afford to relax. She set the cans down and took out two glasses she'd brought for the occasion, and in that moment she realized that she could feel a strange and unfamiliar sensation in her heart, one that felt almost like...

Hope.

Hope for a better future, and for love.

Making her way back to the door, she looked outside and saw that Michael was gathering some more firewood from the edge of the clearing. For a few seconds she watched him working, but after a moment she spotted something moving in the darkness of the forest; she told herself that she was imagining things, yet the movement persisted and she felt a growing sense of dread as she realized that something – perhaps two or three things – seemed to be slowly stalking toward Michael, approaching him from three different sides almost as if -

"Michael!" she shouted, causing him to turn and look at her just as the first wolf began to emerge. "Behind you!"

Michael turned, but in that moment the first wolf rushed at him, slamming into his chest and knocking him down. Two other wolves quickly followed, grabbing at his limbs and starting to pull wildly. Lisa immediately rushed down the steps and hurried across the clearing, before stopping as she saw that the ferocity of the wolves' attack was increasing with each passing second; she watched as Michael tried to pull away, and she was horrified to see blood gushing from a wound on the side of his neck.

"Lisa!" he gasped, as more blood ran from his lips. "Run! Get back inside! Get out of -"

Before he could finish, one of the wolves – the same creature with one eye that Lisa had seen before – bit down hard on his shoulder, bringing a scream from his throat. Lisa froze for a moment, trying to work out how to save him, and finally she realized that she only had one chance.

She turned and ran, racing back to the steps and into the cabin. Almost tripping and falling, she somehow managed to stay on her feet as she raced up the staircase and grabbed her rifle. Checking that it was loaded as she hurried back down, she stumbled out of the cabin and ran across the clearing, finally stopping as she saw that Michael was still on the ground as the wolves ripped and tore at his body. Raising the rifle and aiming, Lisa tried to find a clear shot but she knew there was a risk she'd hit Michael instead. Finally she raised the rifle and fired once into the air, causing the wolves to pull away from their attack from a moment and turn to face her.

"Leave him alone!" she snarled, aiming at the one-eyed wolf as it edged closer. "Get away!"

The wolf began to snarl, and Lisa instinctively fired, hitting one of the wolf's front legs and causing it to slump down as it let out a cry of pain.

With the other two wolves already approaching, Lisa fumbled for a moment as she reloaded the rifle. As soon as she was ready, she turned and aimed at the second wolf, firing a shot that only missed at the last second as the target darted out of the way. She quickly aimed at the third wolf, missing this one as well, but already the three creatures were starting to retreat. The one-eyed wolf, heavily wounded and limping as blood poured from a hole in its leg, limped away into the undergrowth, leaving Lisa to once again reload the rifle before hurrying over to Michael and dropping to her knees.

"Michael, can you hear me?" she stammered, trying to roll him over before letting out a shocked gasp as she saw his bloodied, lacerated face, with chunks of flesh missing all down one side of his cheek and neck. "Michael!" she screamed, desperately searching for a pulse but finding nothing in the mess of torn flesh. "Come back! Michael!"

CHAPTER NINETEEN

Today...

"LET'S STICK TO THE facts," John said firmly, having finally taken a seat in the interrogation room. "At some point this evening, a person or persons unknown broke into McGinty's in town and stole some money as well as an expensive bottle of liquor. I need to find out who's responsible."

"Are you going to look me in the eye?" Nick asked, watching as his father looked through some more paperwork.

"Please just answer the question," John replied, glancing at him very briefly before looking down at the papers again.

"Are you serious?" Nick asked, before looking up at the ceiling just as the lights briefly flickered. "Hey, your generator seems to be -"

"Answer the questions, Nick," John said firmly.

"I'm impressed you're not calling me Nicholas," Nick continued, apparently slightly amused by his father's line of questioning. "Don't you remember what you were like when I was a kid? If I'd been good you always called me Nick or Nicky, but by God when I'd been bad it was always Nicholas. So why the difference now? Why are you calling me Nick?"

"Where were you this evening?"

"Let's see," Nick replied. "I was supposed to meet my father at the bar, but he couldn't be bothered to show up. I waited a while, then I tracked him down at his place and we had an awkward and rather stilted conversation. Then I went back to my motel room and had something to eat before figuring that I might as well get an early night and hit the road first thing in the morning."

"Do you have anyone who can vouch for your whereabouts?"

"Well, I didn't pick up a hooker on my way back to the room, if that's what you mean," Nick said through gritted teeth. "Hey, does Sobolton even *have* hookers. Things seem a little clean-cut around here for that sort of thing."

"Did you break into McGinty's?"

"Do you have any evidence that suggests I

did?"

"Answer the question."

"Or is it all circumstantial?" Nick continued. "I think I get where you're coming from. You think leopards don't change their spots."

"Ten years ago you were involved in an armed robbery at a store in Brooklyn," John reminded him as he turned to another page in the file. "You stole some money from the store's back room, and on your way out you also helped yourself to some of the more expensive items on the shelves."

"And you think that's similar enough to what happened at McGinty's to haul me in," Nick replied. "So how exactly do you think my thought process went? Do you think I got mad at you after our little talk earlier, so I went and recreated my moment of ultimate shame? And do you think that's a coincidence, or did I do it to send you some kind of message?"

"Are you admitting that you were behind the break-in tonight?"

"I don't know, Dad," he sneered. "*Am* I admitting that?"

"If you won't give me a straight answer," John replied, "I'll have you thrown into a cell until morning, and then we can try this again."

"Isn't it kind of unprofessional for you to conduct this interview?" Nick asked. "Isn't there some kind of conflict of interest? Shouldn't you -"

"Answer the goddamn questions!" John snapped angrily, finally meeting his gaze properly. "This is an official police interrogation and you'll tell me what you did!"

"You don't seem to be recording the conversation," Nick pointed out. "Is that -"

"Did you break into McGinty's tonight?"

"Why would I?"

"Because it's right up your alley," John continued, visibly starting to lose control. "You've done something like this before, and it's awfully suspicious that it all happens again right now, just after you show up in town. I don't know if you're trying to embarrass me, but you need to realize that I can't pull strings to get you out of trouble. If you've done this again, you're going to be going back to jail and this time there won't be anything I can do to help you. And even if there was, I wouldn't do it. I'm sick of cleaning up your messes. You're a goddamn idiot!"

"Careful," Nick replied. "That professionalism seems to be slipping."

***

"Goddamn stupid little..."

Stopping at the end of the corridor for a moment, John stared at the wall and considered punching a hole straight through the plasterboard. He even clenched his right fist, ready to strike, but at the last second he managed – as usual – to get his emotions under control. For so long now he'd worked hard to keep a lid on anything chaotic in his life, but it had taken his son less than twenty-four hours to bring all the anger and rage rushing back.

"Heard about your boy, John," he remembered one of the other cops in New York saying. "Man, that sucks. He's sure not a chip off the old block, is he?"

"Stupid little fool," he muttered now, before swallowing hard. He'd had to leave the interrogation room for a moment to pull himself together, but he knew that his son would already have seen the worst.

After all, Nick had always known exactly how to push the right buttons and make John Tench mad as hell.

"Boss?"

Startled, he turned and saw that Carolyn was standing in the doorway that led through to the little staff kitchenette. The front of her shirt was stained with some kind of brown substance.

"I left," she explained, "but then I... I realized I'd forgotten something, so I... I came back and..."

Her voice trailed off.

"Then I was going to make myself a quick

coffee," she continued, looking down at the stain on her shirt, "but that machine has had a mind of its own lately. I swear, the spout just flicked up and sprayed me. Tommy had the same thing happen to him the other day. I don't know what's wrong with the damn thing, but... Well, I guess it's not that important right now."

"Everything's fine," John said, beyond humiliated as he realized that she'd seen him angry. At least, he told himself, he hadn't given in to the urge to punch the wall. "I was just dealing with something and I stepped out to take a look, and to consider something and..."

Now it was his turn to fall silent.

"Are you okay?" Carolyn asked.

"Of course," he replied quickly. Too quickly. "Why do you ask?"

"Well..."

She looked down at his right fist. He looked too, and he immediately unclenched the fist.

"I know I might be speaking out of turn," Carolyn said cautiously, "and I totally get it if you tell me to mind my own business, but I know that's your son in room one. I also know that... well, families can get pretty complicated. Plus you're new up here in Sobolton, and I know you've already made a few friends with Doctor Law and stuff, but if you ever needed to talk to someone and... I don't know, get a female perspective, I'm around most of the time. In fact, I'm usually pretty free, especially in the evenings."

Not really knowing how to respond, John simply stared back at her for a moment.

"Forget it," Carolyn said with a nervous smile, shaking her head. "I'm sure that was a really dumb idea. You've got everything under control, you don't need me to start chiming in with a load of useless opinions. I just figure that you've been under a lot of stress lately and that's got to start coming out somewhere, and I thought I could help relieve you. Your stress, I mean." She sighed. "I know my job is basically just answering the phone," she added, "but when I'm not sitting behind that desk, I can be really bad at talking."

"You're doing just fine," he replied. "Thank you for your concern, but I've got everything under control. The suspect in room one isn't being very cooperative, so I think he might be best off reconsidering his attitude in one of the cells for the night. I'll get Hodges to throw him in one, and then I can get out to the pylon and do something a little more useful."

"A cell?" Carolyn hesitated, before looking along the corridor toward the door to room one. "But... isn't that your -"

"The law's the law," John said firmly, "and there's no doubt in my mind that he's the one who broke into McGinty's. I might not be able to prove it just now, but once the power's back on I'll have a lot more resources at my disposal. Until then, he can sit and rot and think about what he's done. He doesn't get a free ride."

"I'm so sorry, John," she replied, with a hint of tears in her eyes, before stepping closer and putting a hand on the side of his arm. "Like I told you earlier, if you ever need to talk, you know where to find me."

"Thank you, but that won't be necessary," he said firmly. "And now, if you'll excuse me I need to find Hodges, and then I'd better get out to that pylon and see just how they're getting along. The sooner we have the power back on in this town, the sooner we can start getting things back to normal. Or some semblance of normal, at least."

CHAPTER TWENTY

1984...

STILL ON HER KNEES, with the rifle resting on her lap, Lisa continued to stare down at Michael's bloodied corpse. Neither of them had moved now for what felt like an eternity; in reality only five or six minutes had passed since Lisa had finally stopped searching for a pulse, but now – as a cold wind blew across the clearing and the flames of the fire flickered over by the cabin – Lisa couldn't bring herself to tear her gaze away from the bloodied heap on the ground.

The wolves had ravaged Michael's body for only two or three minutes before getting scared off, but in that time they'd almost torn him apart. One of his arms had been nearly ripped away, exposing the bone, while the right side of his face was barely recognizable as human, instead looking like a mismatching mess of crisscrossing cuts and bloodied chunks. Fresh blood had pooled in some of the deeper cuts, quivering in the breeze and occasionally escaping to dribble down what remained of his cheek. The sight was bloody and meaty, yet also devoid of all life.

And deep down, in her horrified state, Lisa knew that he was dead.

Finally, barely thinking at all, she stumbled to her feet. She was trembling all over and she felt sure that she was going to collapse at any moment, and after a few seconds the rifle fell from her hands and landed harmlessly on the ground. Although she knew that she'd need to be able to defend herself if the wolves returned, Lisa couldn't bring herself to care, and in some way she realized that she *wanted* them to come back; at least that way she might be able to join Michael, to follow him out of this world filled with pain and hatred. She'd known him for such a short, precious time, but already she couldn't bear the thought of being without him.

Suddenly she turned, looking back toward the cabin as tears filled her eyes; the first tear quickly ran down her cheek, but she told herself she had to somehow try to hold all the emotion back. A moment later, spotting movement out of the corner of her eye, she turned just in time to see that one of the wolves had returned to watch her from the depths of a nearby thicket.

"You want some more?" she whispered.

Feeling the rage starting to build, she picked the rifle up and reloaded, and then she stormed past Michael's corpse and took aim.

"You want some more?" she screamed, firing and missing the wolf by inches as it turned and bolted away. "I'm right here!" she shouted as loud as she could manage. "If you want some more, come and take it!"

She spotted another wolf. Turning, she fired again, hitting the beast on its flank and causing it to yelp with pain as it scurried away.

Grabbing the last of her ammunition, she reloaded one last time as she stormed past the edge of the clearing and into the forest, still looking around for some sign of the pack.

"Where are you?" she yelled. "Come out, you cowards! Come and finish what you started!"

Suddenly sensing movement nearby, she turned and fired, hitting only a tree.

"Why are you running now?" she shouted, as more and more tears ran down her face and she felt the rage starting to burn in her chest. "Get back here! Get back here and face me!"

She aimed again, and then – once more spotting movement out of the corner of her eye – she turned and screamed as she fired her last shot.

***

The fire was almost dead now, having dwindled over the course of a few hours until there was little more than a scattering of dying embers. Lisa, sitting hunched at the top of the steps outside the cabin's front door, had been watching for a while as the flames had retreated. Now, with darkness having fallen, the last orange glow finally gave up the ghost.

Although she had the rifle next to her, Lisa knew that it was no use now. She was all out of ammunition and, besides, she no longer had the strength to fight. She'd raged for so long in the forest, daring the wolves to return even though she knew she couldn't defend herself; in truth she'd been baiting them, perhaps even *wanting* them to launch one final attack. She knew that they'd have been able to rip her to shreds, just as they'd done to Michael, but she'd told herself that at least she'd be able to make them pay in the process. Instead they'd slunk away, injured but alive, and she couldn't help but think of them somewhere out there in the forest with dried blood around their jaws.

Michael's blood.

Finally she did what she'd been putting off: she looked over at the bloodied corpse on the other side of the clearing, and in her mind's eye she could already see his ravaged flesh. With tear tracks still drying on her cheeks, she stared at him for a moment longer before slowly getting to her feet. Feeling as if her knees might buckle at any moment, she kicked the rifle aside and stumbled into the darkened cabin, and she began to shiver as she felt the night air already cooling. She knew she should leave and head back to town, but at the same time she figured that she might as well just stay at the cabin forever. At least that way, she'd always be close to Michael.

Sitting on the staircase, she looked out once more through the front door. Even in the growing darkness, she could just about see his body on the ground. In that moment, she realized that she had no idea what to do next; she figured that she should tell someone what had happened, but she didn't know anything about Michael really, not even his surname. She had no idea how she'd even begin to explain everything that had happened, and she hated the idea of sitting at some interview table while Joe Hicks and probably also her father watched from the other side. How could she ever make them understand how important Michael had been to her?

Looking down at her hands, she saw that they were shaking wildly. And then, looking outside again, she saw something impossible.

Michael was moving.

"What the -"

Leaping to her feet, she hurried to the doorway and stopped. Her mind was racing and she told herself that she had to be wrong, but Michael's corpse was definitely starting to shift. Worried that something had come to try to pick his bones clean, she picked up the unloaded rifle and began to make her way across the clearing, but as she got closer she realized that somehow – against all the odds – Michael was starting to sit up all by himself, as if somehow he was managing to fight back through death itself.

"Michael?" she gasped, edging closer, still not quite able to believe what she was seeing. "What -"

Suddenly he turned to her, glaring with his one remaining good eye. He was still horrifically injured, with blood running from the various wounds on his face, and for a few seconds he seemed confused until finally he managed to open his mouth.

"Lisa," he groaned, barely able to get any words out at all. "Run!"

"You're alive!" she stammered.

"Run!" he snarled. "I don't want you to see this!"

"I have to get you to the hospital," she said, setting the rifle down and then kneeling in front of him, reaching out to touch his bloodied face but worried that she might hurt him. "Michael, you need -"

"Run!" he screamed, as bones began to crack loudly beneath his flesh. "You can't see this! This is how it always happens, but you can't be here for it!"

"Michael -"

"Go!" he shouted, reaching out with a damaged arm and trying to push her away. Already, the sound of snapping bones had become louder and his back was starting to hunch. "Get out of here before it's too late!"

"Michael, I'm taking you to the hospital," she replied, her voice trembling with shock. "I'm going to have to call an ambulance from somewhere, but -"

"I warned you!" he hissed, tilting his head up until the moonlight caught what was left of his face. "Why wouldn't you listen? There's still time! You have to run and don't ever look back!"

"What are you talking about?" she asked, still trying to work out how she was going to fetch help, but worried now that Michael's mind was broken. "Michael, I don't know what's happening but we have to get you to the Overflow and then -"

"Run!" he screamed one last time, before opening his mouth wide as the skin on his face began to split open.

"Michael?" Lisa sobbed, with fresh tears running down her face. "What -"

Before she could finish, his face broke apart and something else began to emerge from beneath, something inhuman, something simultaneously strange and familiar. Staring in horror at the nightmarish sight growing in the moonlight, Lisa saw that two dark, angry eyes were pushing out from inside his head, accompanied by what appeared to be the long, wet and bloodied snout of a wolf. As the rest of Michael's human face sloughed off to the sides and the wolf snarled, Lisa saw a huge set of fangs dripping with saliva; at the same time, she heard bones splitting and snapping all through his body as he continued to writhe and shift.

Finally, as the emerging wolf began to snarl at her in the moonlight, Lisa could only scream.

CHAPTER TWENTY-ONE

Today...

"DAD, YOU HAVE TO get me out of this," Nick sobbed frantically. "I didn't mean to do anything wrong, I swear. It was all a big mistake! Dad, please, help me!"

Suddenly someone knocked on the cruiser's window, breaking John out of his memory and forcing him to turn and look outside. He quickly wound the window down and saw Abe Landseer leaning down to him in the moonlight.

"Sorry," John muttered, annoyed that he'd been disturbed by thoughts of something that had happened so many years earlier, "I would have been here sooner but I'm afraid I got caught up in a few things in town."

As Abe stepped back, John opened the door and climbed out of the cruiser.

"I can imagine," Abe muttered. "People can be feral when the power's off, can't they? I see it all the time."

"How are things going out here?" John asked, still slightly worried that he'd forgotten something. He looked over at the pylon and saw that several figures were still working high up. "Are we any closer to getting the power back on?"

"We're real close," Abe told him as they began to make their way across the grass, heading over to the trucks parked near the pylon's base. "Actually, over the past few hours we've managed to make some great progress. I'm confident that we'll have your town all hooked back up well before morning."

"That would be good," John said, stopping and looking up at the workers high above.

"Got much of a head for heights?" Abe asked.

"I can mange," John admitted, "but I can't say that I envy you and your team too much." He paused, before turning to see Toby and Sheila standing a little further, each still holding a rifle. "How about the wolf situation? Have they been back to bother you again?"

"Nothing so far," Abe told him. "I've got to admit, it's been good to have your two guards here.

Otherwise I think some of the team might have walked."

"There really aren't supposed to -"

"There aren't supposed to be wolves anywhere near Sobolton," Abe replied with a chuckle. "Yeah, everyone's heard that story. I think some even believe it too. Not in my line of work, though. Did you know that our department has had to send crews out to this particular stretch on thirteen occasions in the past thirty years alone?"

"Is that a lot?"

"Is that a lot?" Abe said, parroting his question. "It's way above the average. And you know, people talk. It's never just simple damage out here, it's always something far more substantial. If you ask me, someone or something in this neck of the woods *really* doesn't like the fact that we've got these power-lines in place. Every so often they decide to take a swipe at them."

"I've been thinking the same thing," John admitted. "It's such a remote location, though. I'm really not sure what more we can do to keep it all safe. Short of -"

"Dad, help me!" Nick yelled. "Dad, please!"

Startled, John turned and looked back toward the cruiser. For a moment he genuinely believed that Nick might be nearby, but after a few seconds he realized that once again he'd been spooked by nothing more than a memory. Ten years later, he was still sometimes reliving that awful night when he'd been called to the station by concerned colleagues, only to see his own son getting dragged away. At first he'd assumed that there must be a mistake, that Nick couldn't possibly have been involved in a robbery, but over a few hours the truth had finally dawned. Ever since then, John had known that his son was no good.

And once again, Nick was in a police cell, this time in Sobolton.

"Sheriff Tench?"

"We're going to stick around until you guys are done," John said firmly, snapping back to the present day as he turned to Abe once more. "I'm going to be here personally. This town has suffered long enough and the time has come to get the power back on."

***

"Haven't seen so much as a blade of grass blowing in the wind," Toby muttered a short while later, leaning against the side of John's cruiser. "Haven't heard so much as the rustle of a critter in the grass."

"Honestly," Sheila said, "it's been completely quiet out here. I'm pretty sure any wolves are long gone."

"Let's hope that's the case," John replied, still watching as the team worked on the pylon. He

ELECTRIFICATION

paused for a moment, lost in thought, trying to avoid thinking about his son again.

"Boss, are you okay?" Sheila continued.

John turned to him.

"You just seem... thoughtful."

"Do you ever feel like you've forgotten something?" John asked. "I've got this nagging sense in the back of my mind that there's something I should have done, and I just didn't do it."

"Like when you worry you've left the stove on?" Toby asked.

"Something like that."

"I know what you mean," Toby continued, nodding gently. "If I'm leaving the house for more than a day, I always take a photo of the stove right before I leave, on my phone. That way I can check it later and prove to myself that the whole house isn't likely to burn down while I'm gone."

"Smart," Sheila muttered. "I might try doing that."

"Hey," John said, pointing past them, "do you see that light?"

Toby and Sheila both turned, and for a moment the three of them stared into the darkness. Far away, off in the distance, a single little light could just about be seen burning in the void.

"Huh," Toby said after a moment. "I didn't notice it until now. That must be way, way out from the town, though. It'd be somewhere past the lake."

"Wouldn't it be more to the west?" Sheila asked. "If you think where we are now, that light must be on the other side of Cutter's Hill."

"Wherever it is," Toby added, "it's buried way deep in the forest."

"Anyone got any idea what it could be?" John asked.

"Could be one of the old logging cabins," Toby suggested. "There are a few of the out there, and I think sometimes people use them when they're off hunting or fishing. They're not supposed to, of course, but it's not like anyone's gonna stop them. There's a map somewhere at the station, shows where they all are." He turned to John. "Why? Are you gonna storm out there and chuck them out?"

"It just looks odd, that's all," John replied, "and -"

Before he could finish, the light abruptly vanished, as if it had been snuffed out.

"And there it goes," Toby chuckled. "As quickly as it appeared."

After watching the distant darkness for a moment, John took a couple of steps forward. He waited for a few seconds, in case the light might reappear, and deep down he had no idea why he was so interested. And then, looking at the almost pitch-black treeline ahead, he realized that he could just about make out the dead little girl watching him from the shadows. He immediately opened his mouth to call out to her, before stopping himself just in time as he worried that the others might think he'd completely lost his mind.

"Wait here," he said finally, checking that he had his gun before starting to make his way toward the trees.

"Did you see something?" Sheila called out. "Did you see a wolf?"

"Not a wolf!" he called back to her. "Stay where you are and keep a lookout. This is something else entirely."

As he started to jog across the grass, he realized that the girl hadn't moved at all. The closer he got to her, the more he felt as if her eyes were burning into him, until finally he stopped just a few paces short of her position and found himself meeting her gaze directly. For a moment he worried that even by speaking, he might cause her to vanish, but he couldn't shake the feeling that she must have appeared to him for a reason. She obviously wanted something.

"What is it?" he asked, keeping his voice low just in case anyone back by the cruiser might hear him. "Why can't you just tell me?"

He waited, but she simply stared back at him as if she expected him to automatically understand.

"Can't we just cut to the chase?" he continued. "I think we've established by now that

I'm not very good at riddles or puzzles. I'm sorry, but you're going to have to be a little more direct. What is it that you want me to do?"

Again he waited, and he realized quickly that he needed to try a new approach.

"Okay," he continued, "listen, Eloise -"

As soon as that name had left his lips, the girl turned and ran, racing away through the trees and disappearing into the forest.

"Wait!" he called out, hurrying after her before he even had a chance to wonder whether he might be making another terrible mistake. "Eloise! Slow down!"

CHAPTER TWENTY-TWO

1984...

"LISA? LISA, HONEY, IS that you? Again?"

Opening her eyes, Lisa saw the soft morning blue of the sky. A moment later a figure stepped into view, staring down at her, and Lisa blinked several times as she found herself looking up at the concerned face of her neighbor Stacy Abermayer.

"Now, Lisa," Stacy continued, "you know me. I'm not judgmental, and we were all young once, but don't you think this is starting to get just a little ridiculous? There's nothing wrong with going out and enjoying yourself every so often, but you have to learn your limits. If you keep drinking until you pass out, one of these nights you're gonna get yourself into a lot of trouble."

Sitting up, Lisa tried to remember what had happened. Looking around, she saw that she was once again on the sidewalk near her father's house. She could feel a throbbing ache in the back of her head, and she felt as if all her memories were mixed up in some kind of mass in her head that refused to give up its secrets. She could hear Stacy Abermayer still talking, but somehow the woman's voice was unable to break through the deafening silent scream in her head. She furrowed her brow, trying to concentrate, and finally everything came tumbling back all at once.

"I'm no prude, Lisa," Stacy continued, "but you need to realize that you can have fun without ending up in this kind of state. I mean, seriously, what's your father gonna say?"

***

"Okay, Lisa, calm down," Rod said, holding his hands up as he turned to her in the kitchen. "You're giving me a headache with all the -"

"Dad, I know how it sounds but I swear I'm not making it up!" Lisa sobbed, with flecks of dirt and mud still dried across her face, and her damp clothes hanging from her body with thick tears in places. "Can you please just listen to me and try to understand that it all really happened?"

"Here's what you need to do," he replied

with a heavy sigh. "Go upstairs and get changed. Take a long, hot bath and just try to... soak for a while. And then when you get back down, I'll have some breakfast for you. There's another power cut so it won't be anything fancy, but I can rustle something up. We can talk then, or perhaps you should get some sleep and then we'll talk when I get back from work. The point is, you look like an absolute mess and you're clearly in no fit state to -"

"He changed," she stammered, cutting him off. "Why aren't you listening to me, Dad? Michael changed, right in front of my eyes. It was like his body was twisting and breaking, like it was trying to fix itself, and in the process it was like his skin started to come away and underneath there was this kind of..."

Her voice trailed off for a moment as she thought back to that awful sight in the moonlight. No matter how many times she tried to tell herself that she was wrong, that she'd imagined the whole thing, she knew exactly what she'd seen: somehow the head of a wolf had begun to burst out from beneath Michael's own face, and his body had been changing too. She remembered falling back against the ground as he'd leaned toward her, she remembered the snarl coming from his jaws, and then...

And then what had happened?

She wasn't certain, but she worried that she

might have simply passed out. She had absolutely no idea how she could have made it back to the town, although she knew that once Michael had carried her out of the forest. Had the same thing happened now? And if so, how could he have done something like that when he'd been so clearly on the verge of turning into some kind of...

"Wolf," she whispered softly. "A werewolf."

"What did you just say?" Rod asked.

"Dad," she continued, "believe me, I know that I sound like I've completely lost my mind, but I know what I saw. Michael was dead, he'd been ripped apart by those other wolves. He had no pulse. I know how to check something like that, and he was definitely gone. And then a few hours later, he started to change."

"Lisa..."

"But he was hurt before," she added, still struggling to piece everything together. "He wouldn't tell me exactly what had happened, but he'd been hurt and then he got better really fast. What if this is his way of doing that? What if, whenever he's hurt, he can fix it by changing his body? I read a story like that once, it was just some stupid nonsense but what if there was actually a hint of truth to it all?"

"Do you mean those trashy paperbacks you love so much?" he asked, stepping past her and picking up a small pile of books from the counter.

He took a moment to look through the various covers. "I always thought these were bad for you, and now I'm starting to see that I was right. Lisa, you're a smart girl but I think you're forgetting how to tell the difference between fantasy and reality."

"It's starting to make sense now," she told him, clearly lost in thought. "Dad, there are other wolves out there too. What if they're like him?"

Still holding the books, Rod turned to her.

"What if they're all werewolves?" she asked. "What if there's a whole pack of them out there, and Michael's somehow been trying to keep himself separate, but they won't leave him alone? He mentioned having brothers, so what if the wolves that attacked him *are* his brothers and there's some kind of family feud going on?" She thought for a moment longer. "He saved me from them before," she added. "It's all starting to come together. Michael saved me, and the secret he was keeping from me was the fact that he knows those wolves. I kept seeing a wolf that only has one eye, I think that might somehow be the leader of their pack. And for some reason the rest of the pack hates Michael!"

"Lisa -"

"What if it's because of me?" she gasped. "What if they're not supposed to mix with humans, and Michael made them even angrier because of all the time we were spending together? Dad, what if this is all my fault?"

"Okay, Lisa, but -"

"Dad, I think -"

"Lisa, listen to me!" he said firmly, cutting her off. Putting an arm around her, he began to steer her toward the hallway. "Here's what we're going to do. You're going to go upstairs and clean yourself up, and while you're doing that I'm sure your thoughts will calm down. Then, if you really insist on not taking a nap, you can come back down and tell me all about this once you've got it settled in your head."

"What's the point?" she asked. "You think I'm out of my mind."

"I didn't say that," he replied, stopping at the foot of the stairs. "I admit, this has all come out of nowhere. There's still no power, so I was only going to do more painting at the office anyway. I'll take the morning off instead, and we can sit at the kitchen table and you can tell me exactly what you think has happened. But Lisa, please, first I really need you to take a bath and just try to calm yourself down a little."

"And then you'll listen to me?"

"I promise."

She hesitated, before starting to make her way upstairs. She still felt weak, as if she might faint at any moment, and when she reached the top she turned and looked down at him again.

"I'm not crazy, Dad," she said cautiously,

her voice trembling with fear. "Believe me, I know exactly how all of this sounds and I wouldn't have told you about it if I wasn't certain. Michael might still be out there. Do you really promise that you'll listen to me and take it all seriously?"

"You have my word," Rod said firmly. "Hand on heart and hope to die."

Once Lisa had made her way to the bathroom, Rod walked back into the kitchen. He stopped for a moment to look once more at the small pile of paperbacks, and he let out a weary sigh as he saw a succession of bright and garish covers, each depicting a woman locked in an embrace with some kind of supernatural figure. He opened one of the books at random and read a few lines, and then – hearing water starting to run into the bath upstairs – he set the books down and hurried to the phone in the corner.

He dialed a number, and then he glanced over toward the hallway again, just to make absolutely certain that there was no risk he might be overheard.

"Sobolton Sheriff's Department," a voice on the other end of the line said a moment later. "How can I help you today?"

"It's Rod Sondnes here," he replied, speaking softly as water continued to fill the bath upstairs. "I need you to put me though to Deputy Joe Hicks. Tell him it's urgent."

AMY CROSS

CHAPTER TWENTY-THREE

Today...

STUMBLING THROUGH THE BUSHES, John looked around for some sign of the little girl. He could barely see anything at all; the night's strong moonlight struggled to break through into the depths of the forest, leaving nothing more than a few sharply-angled shafts of light that cast strange shadows all around. Turning, John looked back the way he'd just come, but he was already starting to realize that he might be engaged in a pointless chase.

Again.

"Eloise!" he called out, having noticed that she'd run as soon as he'd mentioned that name earlier. "Where are you?"

He waited, still trying to get his breath back, but all he heard was the gentle rustle of leaves high above.

"That *is* your name, isn't it?" he continued. "And I'm not the only person you've been appearing to, am I? I spoke to the guy at the thrift store, he saw you in their storeroom. If you've been there, then I'm willing to bet you've shown up in a few other places around town. You're trying to tell us all something, aren't you?"

Again he waited, but he already felt as if he wasn't about to get any kind of straight answer.

"I'm right here," he said somewhat plaintively. "I'm waiting for you to tell me everything. Can you do that, Eloise? Can you tell me how you ended up in that ice?"

As he turned and looked the other way, he was suddenly struck by the sense that – even if he couldn't see the girl – she was still watching him somehow, perhaps hiding in the shadows.

"There was a wolf involved, wasn't there?" he added. "A wolf carried you, but I don't think the wolf hurt you. It certainly didn't kill you. It's almost as if... I'm starting to think that the wolf was trying to help you. To get you away from danger, at least. If I'm right about that, can you give me a sign. Can you show me the -"

Suddenly he heard footsteps racing closer. He turned just in time to see the little girl racing out from between two trees, clearly terrified as she ran through the forest.

"Wait!" he called out, but she was already disappearing into the shadows again.

"Is that what happened?" he asked. "Eloise, were you chased through the forest? Who was after you?"

Silence had returned now; the footsteps were gone, and while John still clung to his belief that ghosts couldn't possibly be real, in that moment he was willing to consider any possibility. He'd felt for a while now that the little girl was trying to show him something, and that she seemed to be getting frustrated by his inability to catch on, although he was also frustrated by her apparent determination to only reveal the truth in piecemeal fashion, presenting nothing more than brief fragments that he still hadn't managed to fit together.

And then, just as he was about to give up and return to the others, he realized that he could hear a weeping sound coming from somewhere nearby. He looked around, and finally he began to set off across a patch of ground that sloped gently upward, picking his way through thick undergrowth as he edged closer and closer to whoever was sobbing. He had to support himself against the trees as he passed, until finally in the darkness he felt his right foot starting to slip. He took another step forward, then another, before -

Suddenly the girl appeared directly in front of him. John opened his mouth to ask what was wrong, but in that instant she stepped forward and screamed before disappearing into thin air.

Fumbling for his flashlight, John switched it on and aimed it forward. He saw no sign of anyone, but after a few seconds he realized that the ground fell away directly ahead; he took a careful step toward the ridge, and when he looked down he saw that a steep slope fed down into what appeared to be a narrow trench running straight through the forest. The formation looked natural enough, like just another strange contour in a place filled with undulations, but he quickly realized that anyone falling down the slope would possibly end up injured. Robert Law hadn't mentioned any injuries consistent with a major fall, but in that instant John couldn't help but wonder whether the girl had led him to this point for a very specific reason...

Before warning him so that he wouldn't go over the edge.

"You fell," he whispered, trying to fit everything together. "It wasn't bad enough to kill you, it maybe wasn't even bad enough to leave any serious damage, but you fell and..."

He looked over his shoulder, watching the darkness.

"Something was chasing you. You fell, and

that allowed it to catch up. But then how did you end up in the ice? The temperature dropped suddenly that night. I'm no expert, but if that drop was particularly abnormal, it might even have frozen within a few hours."

He looked back down into the deep trench, but once again he felt that he wasn't quite smart enough to figure out every last clue presented by the girl.

"You were being chased through the forest," he said out loud finally. "You fell. You were caught. Then something happened, and a wolf ended up carrying you away, except it didn't get you to safety. Instead, it put you into the lake just before the water froze and then..."

As his voice trailed off, he thought back to one of his very first nights in Sobolton, shortly after he'd officially taken over as the local sheriff. He'd encountered a wolf in the forest and...

"I'm sorry for what you've been through," he remembered saying, "but -"

In his mind's eye, he saw it all again: *the wolf lunged at him, snarling and trying to bite his hand. He pulled the trigger, blasting the animal's face and sending it crashing back down against the ground. A brief, anguished yelp rang out, and John watched in horror as the wolf shuddered frantically against the snow.*

Now, standing in the darkened forest, John

felt as if that wolf had to be part of the story. After all, that particular wolf had been sick, mourning its dead cubs. Was it such a stretch to think that the same wolf would have tried to protect a young girl running frantically through the forest? He thought back to the other figure he'd encountered that night, the man who'd seemingly begun to transform his body before falling through the ice. He'd tried to put that moment out of his mind, to pretend that somehow he'd misunderstood, but deep down his gut was telling him that everything he'd experienced was somehow connected.

"There's a whole other world out here," he said softly now, speaking out loud because at least this way he felt he had a chance of understanding. "A whole world that's separate from the town, and Eloise..."

His voice trailed off.

"Eloise is part of *that* world, not the world of Sobolton. That's why I haven't been able to make much sense of it all. When we found her, she'd crossed over to us, but she came from some other place that exists out here."

"You still don't get it, do you?" Joe's voice sneered in his memory, echoing through from the moment before the wolves had ripped him apart. "John, there are no words that can fix this now. You have to respect the rules of this place, and one of the rules is that -"

"One of the rules," John continued now, "is that you should never cross from one world to the other. Because if you do, you'll end up like..."

Hearing the sound of a twig snapping, he turned and saw the dead girl standing just a few feet away, watching him intently.

"But if you're from another place," he said, staring at her with a growing sense of suspicion, "then what does that make you? Are you somehow one of them?"

He waited, but she simply continued to meet his gaze, almost as if she was encouraging him to complete his thought.

"Your name's Eloise," he said firmly. "I don't know your surname Perhaps you don't even have one, not if you were born out here and you've never really been part of the world of man. But you ran that night, you ran so far and so fast that you ended up in our world, and then all hell broke lose." He paused for a moment, thinking back to the last few times he'd seen the girl's ghostly figure in the forest. "You've been leading me here," he added. "To roughly this same part of the forest, but why? What -"

Before he could finish, she held out her left hand and dropped something onto the ground. Confused, John hesitated for a moment before stepping forward and looking down; he didn't see anything at first, but finally he crouched to get a better look. Digging his hands through the mulchy dirt, he wasn't really sure what to expect, and he almost gave up until after a few more seconds he felt something hard poking out from the soil. He had to dig a little more, but finally he lifted up what turned out to be a small, rusty old-fashioned key. He turned it around in his hand, seeing lots of scratches and marks on the key's surface, and he realized that this was what the girl had been trying to show him for some time now.

"What does it open?" he asked, looking up at her ghostly face, surprised that she hadn't performed another disappearing act.

Slowly, she turned and pointed through the forest, but when he looked in that direction John saw only darkness.

"What does this key open?" he asked again. "It looks old. What was it doing here in the first place? Did you drop it? Those other times I saw you out here, were you trying to lead me to this point so that I could find it? What -"

Suddenly he heard a shot firing in the distance, followed by another and then – as he got to his feet – panicked voices starting to shout out.

"The wolves," he stammered, before turning to see that the girl was still watching him. "I have to go and help them."

She turned and looked into the darkness, as if she still expected him to understand what she was pointing at.

"I'll be back," he added, as he raced away through the forest, determined to reach the pylon and help the others. "Don't go anywhere! I'll be back!"

AMY CROSS

CHAPTER TWENTY-FOUR

1984...

"IT'S BEEN GOING ON for days now," Rod Sondnes said as he sat in the parked police cruiser, watching as more rain fell on the windshield. "At first I thought she'd break out of it, but..."

His voice trailed off.

"It's like it's rooted in her mind now," he continued. "She can't shake it off. She keeps going on about this guy she met out in the forest, this Michael fellow. I knew she was distracted recently, but I kept telling myself that she was finally being a normal teenager. But now she keeps saying that all these crazy things happened, and that..."

Again, he struggled to complete the sentence.

"She says she saw him change, Joe," he added finally. "At least, he was *starting* to change. And when when she describes it..."

His mouth hung open for a few seconds as if he couldn't quite bring himself to contemplate the awful truth.

"She -"

"Now just stop fussing," Joe Hicks replied, sitting in the seat next to him. "What did I tell you, Rod? I know some people who know some people, I'm a very well-connected fellow, and I've managed to pull some strings."

"But -"

"Lakehurst isn't close enough to Sobolton that anyone's gonna recognize her," Joe continued, turning to him as more rain fell. "It's a... I don't quite remember the official term, it's a level four psychiatric evaluation and treatment center or something like that. The point is, there are people there who can help a girl like Lisa, and the good news is that we're catching it early. If you wait, she'll need even more treatment." He paused, watching the side of Rod's face. "You called me for a reason. You called me because you know that I get things done."

"She's my only child," Rod replied, with tears in his eyes. "The thought of sending her away to some -"

"Think of it like a vacation," Joe said firmly,

interrupting him. "What's the purpose of a vacation, Rod? It's to come back refreshed and happy and raring to go again. That's exactly how she's going to be. But the alternative simply isn't something we can contemplate. You know how things work around these parts, Rod. We can't have Lisa, or anyone for that matter, running around rambling on about wolves and... about strange things from the forest. Things only work in Sobolton if we keep a lid on all of that."

"Promise me they won't hurt her."

"I promise," Joe replied. "Lakehurst is a good place. It has a real fine reputation."

"She won't *want* to go," Rod added, watching the house on the other side of the road. "She'll resist."

"That's why I'm here," Joe pointed out. "Your her father, naturally you can't be too tough with her. But I can do whatever's necessary. All you need to do is get out of this car and walk away, and then I'll go and persuade Lisa to come with me. I'll drive her to Lakehurst myself, it'll only take a few hours, and I've already made the necessary calls so they know to expect her. They'll start her treatment immediately, and by tonight she'll be well on the road to recovery." He waited for an answer. "Or we can leave it," he added, "and then we'll just end up in this same position in a week or two from now, except Lisa'll be worse and her treatment'll need to be longer. You want to nip all of this in the bud, don't you?"

"And you're sure we're not doing this too soon? Couldn't we wait?"

"Waiting won't do any good," Joe replied. "How many times do I have to tell you that, Rod? I've seen things like this before. You have to act fast!"

Rod hesitated, before opening the door on his side and stepping out of the cruiser.

"Just get it over with," he said, standing in the rain. "I love her, Joe. I just want her to be happy. Please, don't be too rough with her."

With that, he shut the door and walked away along the street, leaving Joe to peer out at the house.

"Oh, I won't be rough at all," he murmured with a growing smile. "I mean, not unless she gives me no choice."

***

"Let me go!" Lisa gasped several hours later, stumbling away from the cruiser with her wrists cuffed behind her back. "Where's my father? I want to see him!"

"How many times do I have to tell you?" Joe sneered as he made his way around from the cruiser's other side. "Your daddy and I discussed this at length and he agreed that this is what you need."

She turned to him, with a trace of blood still glistening on her cut lip, and then – hearing footsteps – she turned to look at the huge building that stood a couple of hundred feet away. To her horror, she could already see a couple of people emerging from the front door wearing white coats, followed a few seconds later by an older man and a younger woman who appeared to be in charge.

"This is the best thing for you, Lisa," Joe continued. "I know it won't seem like that right now, but you have to understand, you can't keep rambling about werewolves and -"

"I saw him!" she snapped, turning to him again. "I saw Michael change!" She looked at the cruiser. "I need to go back there," she added. "I need to go back to the cabin and try to find him again. None of this makes sense, but I can *make* it make sense, I can figure it all out."

"Or you can let the professionals fix the whole thing for you," Joe suggested. "Doesn't that sound a whole lot easier? You're not the first little girl to show up and -"

"I'm not a little girl!" she hissed, stepping toward him, straining at her handcuffs.

"You're not the first little woman to spout off about stuff like this," Joe replied, not even flinching as he met her gaze. "Certainly not in Sobolton. It happens, every so often. Someone strays where they shouldn't, and they have to be nudged back onto the right path. Which is exactly what the good folk at Lakehurst are going to do. They've got experience in this sort of thing."

"Ms. Sondnes?"

As soon as she heard someone saying her name, Lisa spun around and saw that the figures from the building had finally reached her.

"Lisa Sondnes," the nearest man said with a faint smile, "it's nice to meet you, I've heard a lot about you. I'm Doctor Arthur Campbell and I'm one of the resident clinicians here at Lakehurst. Our mutual friend here, Mr. Hicks, called me and explained a lot about your situation. Now that you're here, I think we're going to make some real progress. I'm absolutely confident that soon you'll be feeling a whole lot better."

Lisa turned to look at the woman standing next to Campbell, and then at the two orderlies who looked like they were ready to drag her away.

"I'm not crazy," she explained, her voice faltering as tears filled her eyes. "Why's everyone acting like I'm crazy, when I'm not? Everything I saw was real, everything happened exactly as I described it. The wolves, the changes, Amanda Mathis in the forest, all of it's real. Why won't anyone believe me?"

"See what I mean?" Joe chuckled as he looked over at Doctor Campbell.

"Let's get you inside, Lisa," Campbell replied, as the two orderlies took hold of her arms from either side. "I've got your treatment plan all worked out."

"No!" Lisa shouted, struggling to pull away, only for the orderlies to hold her more firmly as they began to force her toward the hospital's front door. "Let go of me! Joe, tell them to stop! I don't belong here! There's nothing wrong with me! Joe, tell them to let me go! I want to go home!"

"You'll be home soon enough!" Joe called after her with a grin. "Once you're better."

"Nurse Cole," Campbell said to the young woman at his side, "I see no reason to delay. Take her straight through to the treatment room and get her ready."

"Of course," she replied, before looking Joe up and down for a moment with a disapproving stare, then turning and following the others. "Anything you say, Doctor Campbell."

"What crawled up *her* butt and died?" Joe muttered, although he couldn't help watching Nurse Cole's backside as she walked away. "Snooty bitch."

"We're going to need to keep Ms. Sondnes for at least two weeks," Campbell told him. "Perhaps a little longer. If what you told me is true, this mania might already be quite deep-seated, so we'll need to put her through several rounds of treatment before we have a hope of correcting everything." He paused for a moment. "There's one thing you weren't quite clear about, though. You told me about all her claims, but I really do need to know... to what extent could those claims be said to be true?"

"Well, that's a difficult question to answer," Joe replied. "My old friend told me that you'd be able to stop her saying all this stuff. That's all that matters."

"I can read between the lines," Campbell muttered, checking his clipboard, before turning and heading toward the hospital, where Lisa was being half-dragged kicking and screaming through the front door. "I'll be in touch."

"Take your time," Joe said with a smile, watching as the orderlies lifted Lisa up and forced her inside, with the nurse quickly following. "One day, I'm going to be in charge of things in Sobolton. I'm gonna be the sheriff, and that's when things are really gonna get sorted. No-one's gonna be complaining or causing trouble when *I'm* the boss."

CHAPTER TWENTY-FIVE

Today...

"OVER THERE!" TOBY YELLED, aiming his rifle toward the dark treeline. "I saw -"

"It's me!" John shouted, emerging from the shadows with his hands up. "It's only me!"

"We saw two of them, at least," Sheila said breathlessly, hurrying over to him. "They were trying to make their way round past the cruiser, it was like they were stalking the guys working on the pylon."

"I'm pulling my men out right now," Abe said firmly. "We can't work in these conditions."

"Just hold on for one moment," John replied, looking past the cruiser and watching out for any hint of the wolves' presence. "Are you sure it was them? Did you actually see -"

"It was two wolves," Toby replied before he could finish. "John, they were big bastards, and I don't think they're very scared of us. I fired a warning shot and they didn't take off or bolt of anything like that. If anything, they just seemed annoyed that we'd noticed them."

"They were hunting," Sheila added.

John turned to her.

"You could just feel it," she continued. "It was in the way they were moving, it was in the way they were doing everything. It was like they were moving as quietly as they could, and they were getting ready to pounce."

"Everyone down!" Abe yelled at the men still high up on the pylon. "We're done here!"

"No," John replied, "just wait a -"

"I'm not putting my men in danger," Abe replied, turning to him. "Do you think we even wanted to come out here in the first place? Everyone's heard about Sobolton, everyone knows that something vandalizes the pylons here and that there's something just not right about it. I'm no expert, I couldn't tell you a damn thing about any of it, but even *I* know that Sobolton's the kinda place no-one wants to go, not if they're in their right mind. Even that motel we get put up at, that run-down shit-hole at the edge of your town doesn't feel right. I'm sorry about whatever's going on here, I really am, but I'm not gonna put my team in danger just so you lot can get your power back."

"I want everyone to calm down," John replied, "and -"

"There!" Toby shouted, turning and aiming past the cruiser. "Damn it, now there are three of them!"

Looking past him, John realized that three large wolves were emerging from the forest and making their way toward the bottom of the pylon. The workers were still climbing down, and the wolves seemed to be creeping closer so they could attack when they were down.

"They're not scared at all," Sheila pointed out. "I've never seen wolves that are so brave."

"Then let's show them what they're dealing with," Toby hissed, taking a moment to adjust his aim and then letting out a shot that rang loudly through the night air.

One of the wolves turned and glanced at him, more irritated than afraid, while the other two showed no reaction at all and simply continued to advance toward the base of the pylon.

"That's not right," Toby stammered. "That's

not normal at all."

"Okay," John replied, "we've tried warning shots. Now let's -"

Before he could get another word out, Sheila pulled the trigger on her rifle. She hit the flank of the nearest wolf, causing it to drop down immediately.

"Got the bastard!" she exclaimed, turning to John. "One down, two to go."

"I'm not so sure about that," Toby added. "Look!"

Already, the supposedly injured wolf was hauling itself up and showing no obvious sign of an injury. Electric lights stood all around, hooked up to generators, and John saw that the wound on the wolf's flank already looked to be healing; even though he knew that what he saw was impossible, he couldn't deny that the wolf appeared to have been barely slowed at all despite taking a direct shot.

"Bring them down!" he barked. "Get closer if you have to, but I want all three of those wolves put out of action."

"Stay up there!" Abe yelled, warning his men to not get any closer to the ground, with one of the wolves already looking up at them from the base of the pylon. "Don't get near them!"

With the others right behind, John began to advance toward the wolves. His heart was racing and he told himself that no wolf could withstand a shot at such close range, but as he raised his hand and took aim, he couldn't shake the feeling that these particular wolves seemed larger and stronger than any he'd seen before; he also knew that he was far from an expert, and he reminded himself that in the cold light of the following morning everything would probably start to make sense.

In that moment, Toby fired another shot, hitting one of the wolves in the neck. The beast turned and snarled, and John saw that it was missing one of its eyes; he felt a shudder run through his bones as he realized that this was one of the wolves that had ripped Joe Hicks to pieces.

He adjusted his aim again and fired, shooting the same wolf in the flank. This time the creature pulled back a little, clearly in pain but not obviously in any kind of bad way; the wolf snarled at its attackers as if trying to warn them off, and nearby one of the others was already trying to climb up the pylon and reach the workers.

"Nothing stops them," Sheila stammered. "I don't get it, they should be dead by now. How are they *not* dead?"

"I don't know," Toby added, already having

to take a moment to reload, "but everything dies if you shoot it enough!"

The one-eyed wolf had already turned and resumed its slow walk to the pylon. John took a moment to aim, and for a fraction of a second he remembered the sight of that same wolf tearing into Joe's body and crunching through the dying man's bones. He'd felt no great love for Joe, but he knew that no man deserved to meet such an awful fate, and he also knew that this beast was a man-killer, which meant that as sheriff he had a duty to bring it down so that everyone else was safe. Finally he fired, hitting the wolf in the side of the head and sending it slumping down onto its side.

"I think you got it!" Sheila shouted.

"I'm not so sure about that," John replied, as the wolf hauled itself back up and turned to snarl at him once more.

The other two wolves turned as well, and now all three began to stalk toward the spot where John and the others were trying to stand their ground. Realizing that something had changed, and that the wolves were now focused on him and his two colleagues, John shot another few rounds but saw that the wolves were completely untroubled even as the bullets burst though their bodies. He could see that the shots were doing damage, but the wolves seemed able somehow to repair that damage almost immediately.

"Uh, what do we do now?" Toby stammered, taking a couple of steps back. "Sheriff? Do you have a back-up plan?"

"Just shoot the damn things!" Sheila hissed, stepping forward and firing again, hitting the one-eyed wolf in the face.

The beast let out a cry and briefly pulled back, before turning to her as the damage began to repair itself. Within seconds the creature was making its way toward her again, as if ready to make her pay for having such temerity.

"We can't reload fast enough!" she shouted, fumbling as she tried to pull some ammunition from her pocket. "Sheriff? What do we do?"

"Stay calm!" John said firmly, before raising his gun and firing again, shooting the one-eyed wolf in the flank.

The creature turned and snarled at him, and in that moment another wolf howled somewhere far off in the distance. The one-eyed wolf half turned, as if something about that howl had caught its attention, and then all three animals hurried away, racing across the ground and rushing past the base of the pylon before disappearing into the forest.

"Did we do it?" Toby gasped, as if he could

barely believe what had happened. "We did it! Damn it, it took longer than it should have, but we scared them away!"

"This place is nuts," Abe stammered, wiping sweat from his brow. "I'm gonna talk to my boss when I get back, and I'm telling him I'm *never* coming out to Sobolton again. We'll fix your power, Sheriff Tench. We're damn near done with that already, but after today you'll be lucky if you can ever get another crew out here. Next time your power goes off, you might find that you're on your own."

"We did it," Sheila said with a relieved sigh. "I don't quite know how, but we did it."

"I'm not so sure that we did anything at all," John said, still watching the dark forest in case the wolves returned. "I think something out there called them off."

CHAPTER TWENTY-SIX

1984...

SITTING IN THE CHAIR in Doctor Campbell's office, Lisa fiddled for a moment with the plastic band around her wrist. She saw her name on one side, in Nurse Cole's careful handwriting, and then she slipped it around and saw the printed name of Lakehurst on the other.

"Did you hear my question?" Doctor Campbell asked. "Lisa, do you know that it's rude to ignore a direct question?"

"Do *you* know that it's rude to treat someone like this?" she replied, finally meeting his gaze again. "Do you realize that it's kind of rude to strap someone down and do things to their head?"

"Lisa -"

"I'm not crazy and I don't belong here!" she snapped. "Why don't you understand that? My dad obviously didn't understand what you were going to do to me, he must have been tricked. If you call him and tell him what's going on, he'll come and take me home."

"I've talked to your father extensively," he replied. "He knows exactly what's going on here."

"That's not true!" she said angrily.

"Lisa, you need to accept the reality of your situation. You're here because a lot of people are worried about you. There are people in the world who truly care about you and love you, and they want you to get better. That's exactly what we're going to work on."

"I'm not working on anything with you!"

"I anticipated a degree of resistance from the start," he told her as he made some more notes on her chart. He was always writing notes about her, as if he was working on some kind of book about her life. "In fact, I'd be worried if you didn't try to fight back, at least at first."

"I want to talk to my father."

"Later."

"I want to talk to him now!" she hissed.

"We don't always get what we want, Lisa," he said firmly. "You have to understand that from the moment you walked through the front door here, you entered a treatment plan that has to be pursued to its natural conclusion. There's no hopping off midway through."

"I didn't *walk* through the door," she replied, as she spotted movement outside. She looked at the window and saw two nuns walking across the sunlit lawn. "I was dragged, kicking and screaming against my will." She blinked, and in that moment the nuns were gone. She watched for them to return, and then – figuring that she must have been mistaken – she turned to Doctor Campbell again. "What law gives you the right to hold me here against my will?"

"You've responded well to your treatment so far," he said, peering at the clipboard again, "but I think a higher dosage might be worth trying. We're still well within the margin for error, and you've shown very few negative side-effects so far. In fact, your resilience is remarkable."

"Sorry to disappoint," she sneered, as she saw the hospital's janitor walking across the lawn. Of all the people she'd met at Lakehurst so far, that guy gave her a particularly strong sense of the creeps. "I know you think I'm going to cooperate eventually and just do what you want, but I refuse." She turned to Campbell again. "I still know that every single thing I've told you is true. I also know that I can figure the rest out once I've talked to Michael some more. I was shocked at first, I didn't know how to process what I'd seen, but now I think

I understand. I just need to talk to him."

She waited for an answer, but she could already tell from the expression on Campbell's face that he barely cared about a word she'd just spoken; she'd already figured out that he was one of the most arrogant people she'd ever met, and in her short time at Lakehurst so far she'd come to despise him more than she'd ever despised anyone else on the planet.

Except Joe Hicks, obviously.

"Can I please just talk to my dad?" she asked finally, hating herself for sounding so weak but unable to hold back as tears once again filled her eyes. "I know I can fix all of this if I just speak to him."

"I'm going to make some changes to this afternoon's treatment plan," Campbell replied, adding more notes to the papers on his desk. "You might find the experience a little less comfortable than before, but that's unavoidable. What matters most is that you start to get better soon, Lisa. I'm confident that we're on the right path and I think with a little extra juice we'll be able to push on. I'm afraid I'll be in meetings this afternoon, but my assistant is more than capable of stepping in." He glanced up at her with a smile that was clearly supposed to be reassuring. "You're in safe hands, Lisa. And very soon you'll be back at home in Sobolton, and you can get on with the rest of your life."

***

Pulling on the restraints around her wrists, Lisa immediately knew that – once again – she'd be unable to break free. That realization didn't stop her, however, and she continued to try to escape even as the door opened and a doctor walked into the room.

"Ms. Sondnes?" he said, studying the clipboard in his hands. "I -"

"Just get on with it," she snarled.

"Ms. Sondnes -"

"I said, get on with it!" she hissed. "Are you deaf! If you're really going to do this barbaric crap, then there's no need to stand around talking about it."

"I see that the nurses have put everything in place," he said, stepping around to the other end of the table and looked down at her as she continued to rest flat on her back. "That's good, it means we can jump straight in. Doctor Campbell has told me about your situation, and he's authorized me to use some slightly unusual methods. I realize that might sound scary, Lisa, but he's a brilliant man and I for one would trust him with my life."

"Just do it!"

Taking a deep breath, she told herself that the time had come to prepare for the worst. She felt utterly humiliated and she still believed that a terrible mistake had been made, that her father would never have signed her up for such degrading treatment, but she'd come to accept that no-one was going to listen to her. Everyone at Lakehurst seemed convinced that they knew so much better, and as she felt tears filling her eyes she resolved to at least not give them the satisfaction of crying. Instead she clenched her fists, digging her fingernails into the palms of her hands and trying to use the pain to keep herself calm.

"You're going to be fully awake for today's treatment," he continued, as he took the mouth-guard from a nearby counter. "By order of Doctor Campbell. I must admit, he has a tendency to think outside the box, but it's hardly my place to argue. I'm new to all of this." He stood over her and held out the mouth-guard. "The notes say you've had a few sessions already, so you should know how this goes. You'll find there are some differences, but that's all part of the regimen so there's no need to worry. You're in safe hands, Ms. Sondnes. We're going to get you better and out the front door before you know it."

"They don't believe me," she replied, with fresh tears dancing in her eyes. "They're treating me like I'm crazy, but I'm not."

She dug her fingernails deeper into her palm; the pain was getting worse, but somehow it wasn't enough.

"Ms. Sondnes -"

"They want to stop me talking about all of it," she continued, feeling as if this might be her last chance to get the truth out. "That's what I don't understand. It's as if they don't want anyone to know what's really happening. Everyone acts like the forest around Sobolton's completely harmless, but I know the truth now, I know that there are people and... things... out there. There's a whole other world, but everyone else seems to want to stick their heads in the sand and just pretend things are normal. I guess that's how it's always been. People just want to believe the lies."

"Ms. Sondnes, I -"

"I saw a werewolf," she added, interrupting him yet again. "Don't you think I know how crazy that sounds? I saw my boyfriend... I mean, he wasn't my boyfriend, at least not yet, but I saw him starting to change. I was so scared, and I ran away, but now I realize I have to go back. I have to find out what happened to him, because right now I have no idea. Can you imagine how that feels? I *have* to go back to the forest. To the cabin. I have to show him that I'm not scared of him. I saw a ghost out there too, a woman, but that's not even the most insane part. That's almost a side-story to the whole thing." She took a deep breath. "I need to tell Michael that I understand what's happening to him. I need to tell him that I'm not scared of him. Not now. I've had time to think about it, and I want to ask him more questions."

"Please let me put the mouth-guard in place."

"And if you don't believe me either," she said, "that's fine too, but it's not going to be enough to make me shut up or pretend like -"

Before she could finish, he reached down and forced the guard into her mouth, using a strap to hold it in place. She tried to keep talking, but all she managed to get out were a series of grunts, and finally she leaned back as she realized that she wasn't going to be able to stop him. She could already hear him bringing the equipment closer, and sure enough she felt the pads being attached to the sides of her head. As more and more tears ran from her eyes and rolled down the sides of her face, she heard the man flicking buttons on the machine. He'd told her that things were going to be a little different this time, and somehow she felt she could already feel a much stronger dose coming.

"Here we go," he said, leaning over her. "Let's hope for better results this time."

Through the tears, she could just about see a name-badge on the front of the man's shirt. She blinked a couple of times, and finally she was able to read the name.

Doctor Robert Law.

Suddenly the machine crackled and burst into life, flooding her brain with a burst of electricity so strong that she could only let out a horrified gasp. She didn't remember the previous sessions, but this time she felt as if a powerful charge was rippling through her brain, filling not only her eyes but also her deepest thoughts – even the vestiges of her dreams – and lighting up every neuron and synapse in her brain, flooding her head until every thought and every memory seemed to merge and form one spluttering mass of consciousness. And the sensation only grew, humming louder and louder until she felt as if her skull was about to burst, until she realized that the electrical charge was about to burst through her entire body and explode.

AMY CROSS

CHAPTER TWENTY-SEVEN

Today...

SUDDENLY A LIGHT-BULB EXPLODED in the corner of the bar, shattering and sending glass flying across the room. At the same time, all the other lights came back on properly, and the alarm system let out a deafening beeping sound as it came back online.

"Finally!" Al Burnham sighed, hurrying across the room and typing his code into the box, silencing the alarm. "Hallelujah!"

Turning, he looked across McGinty's and saw that everything was once again how it should be. He'd stayed late to fix the damage from the break-in, but he'd begun to lose hope that the power would be back on before morning; now the bar seemed to positively throb with electricity, as if all the missing juice was now making up for lost time. Wandering to the far end of the bar, Al saw that even the coffee machine was cycling though its menus as it woke from the dead. He pressed a few buttons before figuring that there was no way he'd ever understand; better, he figured to just let the system do its thing.

Grabbing a dustpan and brush, he made his way around the bar and crouched down to start cleaning up the shards of glass from the shattered bulb.

"Back to normal tomorrow, then," he muttered under his breath. "Lord knows, it's about time. If we'd stayed dark any longer, I reckon everyone in this goddamn town would've turned completely feral."

***

"That's how things oughta be," Toby said, standing on the steps outside the front of the station and watching as lights flickered to life all across the town. "It's like we're emerging back out of the dark ages again. It's like the whole town's coming back from the dead."

"We owe Abe and those other guys," Sheila said as she opened the door and made her way inside. "If I'd been one of the workers, I'm not sure

ELECTRIFICATION

I'd have stuck around after the first wolf attack. I sure wouldn't have stayed after they showed up the second time."

"Do you think things'll get back to normal now?" Toby asked, turning to John.

"Define normal in Sobolton," John muttered.

"Good point," Toby added, rolling his eyes. "Still, you never know. We might get there one day. But I'm gonna head home now, unless you need me some more. This has been a long night and I really need to get some sleep." He paused for a few seconds. "Do you think we need to worry about more wolves?" he asked cautiously. "If they're out there, and if they're mean, we should start warning people."

"I'll think about the best way to do that," John told him.

"I swear I hit them," Toby replied. "I don't know why they wouldn't stay down."

"You did good," John said, patting him on the shoulder before heading into the building. "Real good."

"Hey," Carolyn said as soon as she saw John in the reception area. "Looks like the whole town's got power again. I can go and sort out the generator."

"What are you doing here so late?" John asked, puzzled by the sight of her. "I thought you were going home."

"I was," she replied, "but it's been one thing after another since you left. First there was a call about a drunk and disorderly situation out at the cemetery, and then..."

She turned and nodded toward the desk.

"Do you remember that vase of flowers I had on there?"

"I do, as it happens," John told her.

"It's like the vase just decided to move and tip itself straight over the edge. Landed on the floor and shattered, there was water everywhere, not to mention bits of the flowers. It's taken me the best part of two hours to get everything cleaned up and sorted out, but I think I'm finally ready to head home." She stepped past him. "At least the power-cut's over. That's a huge relief."

"What was the drunk and disorderly all about?" John asked as she headed to the door.

"Oh, Matty's dealing with it now," she replied, stopping and turning to him. "I was gonna let him tell you, but... it seems one of the local drunks was responsible for that break-in at McGinty's. He stumbled off and took his loot to the cemetery, but then he got into a fight with one of the other local drunks and the guy from the gas station across the road ended up calling it in. Anyway, the guy we arrested stinks but he confessed and everything. They even found him with this real expensive bottle that he'd swiped. I guess he thought that with the power off, the place was fair game. Some people are just looking for any excuse to cut loose, huh?"

John opened his mouth to reply, before thinking back to the confrontation with his son in the interrogation room.

"So then we let Nick go," Carolyn added, as if she'd read his mind. "We had to. I mean, we couldn't hold him any longer, could we? Russ ran the paperwork."

"Where did he go?" John asked, his voice tense with fear.

"Back to his motel, I guess," she replied. "We didn't really have any grounds to ask him too many more questions. I'm sorry, John, it's been such a crazy night. But that's good news, isn't it? At least now you know Nick didn't have anything to do with the break-in at the bar."

***

"Nick?"

John hesitated at the door to the motel room, before knocking again. He glanced at his watch and realized that most likely his son would be fast asleep now, but he still felt that he had to at least try to talk to him and set things straight; not that he knew how to even start that conversation, of course, and from experience he understood that any talk with Nick would end up going badly, but he figured that he'd made a mistake and he had to own up to that now.

"Nick?" he called out for a second time, and then he knocked once more. "Listen, I know I'm probably the last person you want to talk to right now, but I came down here to apologize. I got it wrong and I'm willing to admit that. Can we at least talk?"

He waited.

Silence.

"Sheriff Tench?" the guy from the front desk said, wandering over from the vending machine. "A little late for you to be here. Or is it a little early? At this time of the night, I'm not even sure. At least we've got the power back on." He held up his haul of candy from the machine. "Do you know how long I had to wait to get my fix of these things? I even tried to plug the vending machine into a generator, but then I stopped because I got worried that I might blow it up and then I wouldn't be able to get them even when the power came on. I think I might have a problem. I think I'm actually addicted."

He glanced at the door.

"Are you looking for this guy? He checked out a couple of hours ago."

"He did?"

"I was on the desk when he left," he replied, before taking a set of keys from his pocket. He fumbled with the lock for a moment, before pushing it open to reveal the empty room. "Hell, when am I *not* on the desk? Between Horace and me, we're here every damn minute of every damn day. Not that we get much time to have actual lives. The guy in this room seemed real keen to get going. To be honest, he seemed almost angry, I think I might even have seen tears in his eyes. Actually, come to think of it, his last name was Tench too. Any relation?"

Staring into the darkened room, John saw that the bed was empty.

"You can take a look around if you need to," the guy said, reaching past him and switching on the lights, then starting to eat his candy as he wandered back to the office. "Just shut the door when you're done," he added. "I've got to change the sheets and stuff soon, but first Papa needs his sugar fix. I might be back in a minute or two, though. I can be spontaneous like that."

Once the guy was gone, John stepped into the room and looked all around. On his way over to the motel, he'd been rehearsing what he was going to say, trying to work out how he was going to get Nick to understand; he'd been so certain that his son was up to his old habits, that Nick had been responsible for the break-in at McGinty's, but now as he stopped at the foot of the bed and looked around again he realized that he'd jumped to completely the wrong conclusion. Sure, he'd had good reason for those suspicions, but he hadn't allowed for even the slightest sliver of doubt. Now, as he felt his legs weaken, he had no choice but to sit down on the end of the bed as he took a long, deep breath.

"Did you break into McGinty's tonight?" he remembered asking his son, and he realized now that his voice had been positively dripping with certainty.

"Why would I?" Nick had replied.

"Because it's right up your alley," he'd continued. "You've done something like this before, and it's awfully suspicious that it all happens again right now, just after you show up in town. I don't know if you're trying to embarrass me, but you need to realize that I can't pull strings to get you out of trouble. If you've done this again, you're going to be going back to jail and this time there won't be anything I can do to help you. And even if there was, I wouldn't do it. I'm sick of cleaning up your messes. You're a goddamn idiot!"

"Careful," Nick had replied. "That professionalism seems to be slipping."

And now he was gone. He'd skipped town just as soon as he could, giving John no time to apologize. In that moment, sitting all alone on the end of the bed, John realized that he could try to call his son and say something, but he quickly reminded himself that yet another gushing rush of words wouldn't solve anything. After all, he and Nick had argued – sometimes face-to-face, sometimes over the phone – so many times over the years, but they'd never actually managed to fix things. If anything, they'd only ended up making it all worse. Sometimes, John figured now, the best approach was simply to accept that there was no fix and move on.

After all, he'd moved to Sobolton to get away from all the troubles of the past. Now the last connection to that past was broken, and he figured that might be best for them both.

"Dad, I know I screwed up," he remembered a panicking Nick saying ten years earlier, "and I'm sorry, but it was a mistake. I got mixed up with the wrong people and I did something really stupid, but you can't let them send me to jail. Dad, I really need you to pull some favors for me here."

"I can't do that," he'd replied.

"Dad, I'm begging you from the bottom of my heart," Nick had continued. "You're my father, and I know we haven't always seen eye to eye, but you can't possibly let this happen to me. Damn it, I'm your son!"

"My hands are tied," he'd explained. "I can maybe get a parking ticket struck off, that sort of thing, but you've gone too far this time."

"You can't even look at me," Nick had pointed out. "Dad, why can't you even look me in the eye?"

Those words hung in John's mind now for a few seconds, as he looked around the grotty little room and imagined Nick hurriedly packing and racing out through the door.

Spotting a piece of chewed gum on the floor, John picked it up. He turned the gun around in his hand, and then he walked over to the desk and dropped the trash into the can next to the chair.

"Alright if I clean?" the guy from the desk asked, stepping into the doorway with a mop in one hand and a box of sprays and bottles in the other. "I'm kind of on a tight schedule."

"Be my guest," John said, feeling more tired than he'd ever felt in his life as he made his way across the room.

"You don't need to look for evidence or anything?"

"I do not," John muttered, stepping past the man and stopping outside the room, looking across the parking lot. "You're good to go."

"So *was* he related to you?" the guy continued. "The surname was the same, and to be honest he looked a little like you."

"He was," John replied, turning to him. "But he's gone now. You can get on with whatever you

ELECTRIFICATION

need to do."

"But -"

"There's nothing else to say," John added. "Please, don't mind me. I'll leave you to finish up in here."

Making his way over to his cruiser, John couldn't shake a sense of finality. As he stopped to take his keys from his pocket, he knew deep down that he'd never see Nick face-to-face again, and he wondered whether their final meeting could have gone differently. At the same time, he reminded himself that from a purely professional point of view he'd had every right to be suspicious. In reality, he'd only been doing his job. Even if he'd managed to talk to Nick, he wouldn't have apologized profusely; he would have admitted that he'd been wrong, sure, but he also would have insisted that he'd been right to consider the possibility? And how would Nick have taken that argument?

Not well.

In which case, he realized, he was probably better off not having the conversation at all. Over the previous ten years, he and his son had argued countless times, exchanging so many angry words. In that moment, he told himself that there was no point adding yet more words to that pile.

Feeling a buzzing sensation, he pulled his phone out and saw Carolyn trying to get through.

"Again?" he said, trying to sound calm and collected as he answered. "Are you never -"

"John, we just got an emergency call," she replied, sounding as if she was on the verge of bursting into tears. "It's... it's about Tommy."

CHAPTER TWENTY-EIGHT

1984...

"OKAY, STEADY THERE," ROD said, holding the car door open. "Take your time."

"I'm not a weakling, Dad," Lisa said, although she was a little slow as she carefully climbed out of the car and looked around. "You don't have to treat me with kid gloves now I'm back from the hospital."

"You're my little girl still," he replied. "You can't blame me for wanting to look after you."

For a moment, feeling a little nauseous, Lisa had to hold her breath as she waited – hoped – for the sensation to pass. She desperately wanted to prove that she was all better now, that whatever had been wrong was now fully fixed, yet the nausea continued for a few more seconds, twisting and churning in her gut before slowly ebbing away and leaving her feeling just a little steadier.

"I'm fine," she told her father finally, managing a faint smile as she looked both ways along the street. "It seems... different, somehow."

"Different? In what way?"

"I don't actually know," she admitted, before spotting a light on the porch of a nearby house. "The power's back on," she added. "It's probably just that. When I left, we were having another blackout."

"Let's hope those are in the past," Rod sighed as he slammed the door shut. "It's good to have you home, Lisa. The past month hasn't been easy. Well, I know I've got no right to complain. I'm sure it was a hundred times worse for you."

"I certainly don't want to ever go back to that place," she told him. "Although to be honest, I think I'm already starting to forget some of the details. My memory's a little -"

"That's fine," Rod said quickly, cutting her off as he took her by the hand and began to lead her toward the house. "The doctor said you shouldn't really try to force it, you need to focus on the future. If that means taking some time to reassess your ambitions, then -"

"I want to go to veterinary school."

"There's plenty of time to think about it."

"No, I'm serious," she continued. "I've been dragging my heels for long enough, but now I really want to put my nose to the grindstone. Besides, you're gonna need someone to take over when you retire for a life of fishing, and someone has to stop you endlessly painting the office pink."

"I happen to think that the pink looks good."

"I know you do, and that's the problem," she replied as they reached the front door. Turning to him, she seemed lost in thought for a moment. "Dad, I don't quite remember everything that happened," she added, "but Doctor... damn it, I don't even remember his name. The point is, I know I must have been real sick for you to have sent me to that place, and I just want to apologize. I'm sure I put you through a lot, but from now on you don't have to worry. I'm going to go to school and work my ass off."

"I'm so proud of you," he said after a moment, clearly on the verge of tears. "I hope you realize that, Lisa. I don't think there's ever been a father in all the world who's as proud of you as I am right now."

"No need to get too mawkish," she told him. "I know I need to rest a little, but I also want to get on with finishing my college application. There's no time like the present, right? But I'm still not quite sure how to phrase certain things. Would you be able to help me?"

"Of course," Rod replied, before spotting movement nearby. He turned to see a police cruiser rolling very slowly past the house, and in that instant he bristled slightly. "Honey, why don't you go inside and make us some coffee? Get your notebook out and I'll join you in a few minutes to get on with writing this thing. I just need to go and... take care of something first."

***

"She's looking well," Joe Hicks said, as Rod climbed into the parked cruiser and pulled the door shut. "That time away must have agreed with her. I thought people who came back from the loony bin usually had a load of twitches, maybe a shaved head, but Lisa's looking better than ever."

"She's fine," Rod muttered, clearly uncomfortable. "I was going to pop by and see you tomorrow."

"Well, then it's lucky I happened to be passing," Joe told him. "I've saved you the trip. So what did they say at Lakehurst, anyway? Do they reckon they've fixed her?"

"She doesn't seem to remember any of the stuff that happened," Rod admitted. "Her memory of the period before she went in are... hazy, and she's not really trying to recover them. Doctor Campbell said he gave her six round of electric shock therapy in total, and he's convinced that she's going to be fine."

"She's not talking about werewolves and stuff like that?"

"Not now."

"That's good!" Joe said, reaching over and patting Rod on the shoulder. "Man, I don't mind admitting that I was worried for a while." He paused, watching Rod cautiously. "We couldn't have her running around gong on about those things," he added, his tone now sounding markedly more serious. "We couldn't have her upsetting the order and balance that's so essential to our little town."

He waited for an answer, but he could tell that Rod wasn't convinced.

"And we nipped it in the bud nice and early," he added finally. "That's the key to these things, you've gotta not put it off and put it off until it all runs out of control. You did the right thing, my friend. With a little help from yours truly, of course."

"I just wish she'd never gone out there into the forest in the first place."

"Well, she did," Joe reminded him. "Can't undo that. But it's sorted now, and I think all we have to do is wait until the dust settles, and then we can all get on with our lives."

"She's ready to go to college."

"Good for her. Get out of Sobolton."

"She's going to come back, though," Rod added. "She doesn't want to leave town, not properly. And she's got her heart set on running the veterinary surgery when I retire."

"Nothing wrong with a family business passing from one generation to the next," Joe told him. "Besides, it'll be good for her to come back. We can keep an eye on her."

"There's no need to do that," Rod said firmly, turning to him. "She's cured now."

"Sure she is," Joe said, nodding slowly. "Sure she is. Best to make sure, though."

"I need to get back inside," Rod replied, opening the door and stepping out of the car. "I'm going to help her with a few things, and just stay close and make sure she's okay."

"Don't worry about a thing, my friend," Joe said with a chuckle. "You know, I'm just so grateful that I was able to step in and help sort it all out. I see it as kind of... a way of preparing myself for the inevitable day when the good people of Sobolton pick me to be their new sheriff. You know that ultimately I care about this town, don't you? The needs of Sobolton are more important than the needs of any one person."

"So you always say."

"And I'm right," Joe added. "You know, when I finally become sheriff one day, people won't know what's hit them. They'll wonder how they ever managed without me." He paused for a moment longer. "Look after your girl, Rod," he continued cautiously. "We're out of the woods with her, but it's important to make sure there are no loose ends. Don't let her do anything that might jog her memory, at least not while the treatment's settling. We wouldn't want to have to..."

His voice trailed off.

"Have to what?" Rod asked.

"I don't know. Try to fix it all again. I don't mind telling you, if the electric shock stuff hadn't worked, I'm really not sure what we'd have tried next. Your little Lisa made a big mistake, she crossed from one world to the next and she started mixing them all together. That never goes well. Let what's out in the forest, stay out in the forest, and let what's here in the town stay in the town. No mixing. Not now, and not ever."

"I should go," Rod said again, shutting the door before hurrying toward his house.

"Yeah, you do that," Joe muttered, leaning back in his seat. "Make sure she doesn't cause any more trouble."

He watched as Rod disappeared from view, and then he sat in silence for a few minutes, contemplating everything that had just happened. Although he wanted to believe that a short stay at Lakehurst had fixed Lisa's mind and resolved all the problems, deep down he couldn't help but worry that they're really just succeeded in delaying things for a while. Glancing around, he made sure that nobody else was watching the house, and then he started the cruiser's engine and began to pull away from the side of the road.

"I've got a bad feeling about this," he said under his breath. "One day, the debt for all of this is gonna come due."

CHAPTER TWENTY-NINE

Today...

"WHERE IS HE?" JOHN snapped, pushing through the double doors and hurrying along yet another corridor at Sobolton's Middleford Cross hospital. "I'm looking for Tommy Wallace. Where the hell is he?"

"John!"

Looking along another corridor, he saw Robert Law waving at him.

"What's going on?" John barked, hurrying in that direction. "The call just said he'd been found and he was hurt. Where is he?"

"He's being assessed," Robert replied, his voice filled with a sense of simmering shock. "He's in good hands."

"I want to see him."

"Not right now."

"I want to see him, Bob!"

"And I told you, not right now," Robert continued, stepping in front of the nearby door to block his path. "John, he needs to be looked at by medical professionals. The only reason *I'm* here is that I came to look for some of my old papers in the archive, and then I heard that someone from the sheriff's department had been rushed here."

"How is he?" John asked. "Is he hurt?"

"He's hurt, John."

"What happened?"

"Someone found him," Robert explained. "I think it was someone walking their dog. They were going past the building where Lisa Sondnes used to live, and they heard a kind of gasping sound. Apparently Tommy was crawling out from somewhere around the side, and... I heard there was a lot of blood, John. A hell of a lot of blood."

"But what happened to him?"

"I don't think anyone knows just yet. Tommy hasn't been able to talk, and there was no weapon found at the scene. Whoever attacked him must have bolted."

"He was just supposed to observe," John replied. "That's all. He had strict instructions to watch the building and look out for anyone suspicious going in or out."

"This is still a rapidly evolving situation," Robert told him. "It's going to take a little more time before we're able to hear from him, but I'm sure we'll start getting to the bottom of it eventually. Tracy's on her way now, she should be here soon. John, I really just think you need to calm down and let the fine doctors here do their work. I know Middleford Cross doesn't have the best reputation, but there are good people here and they'll look after Tommy. The hard part for us is the waiting."

"I want to see him," John said again.

"You probably won't be able to until at least the morning," Robert replied. "John, I need to prepare you, because Tommy's injuries are quite extreme. I believe he's out of immediate danger, but whoever got to him... John, it's like he was attacked by some kind of wild animal."

"A wolf?"

"Why would you -"

Robert hesitated for a moment.

"No," he added finally, "not a wolf, and not a wild animal. I'm sorry to say, John, that this attack was clearly perpetrated by a fellow human being. Although I use that term lightly, because there's not a lot that's human about what happened to Tommy tonight. In fact, in all my years both in the medical profession and working with the sheriff's office, I don't think I've seen anything quite so horrific. These injuries are life-changing, John. Tommy's not going to be able to ever come back to his old position."

"What exactly do you mean?" John asked cautiously.

"When I said it wasn't a wild animal just now," Robert continued, "I'm not sure that's true. I feel like this was a bit of both, John. A wild animal and a man, mixed together. Certainly something that shouldn't be on the streets of our fair little town." He hesitated again, as if he was struggling to work out exactly what to say next. "John, I think I need to come clean about something. I've been completely honest with you since you came to Sobolton, but tonight has made me realize that I've perhaps held back on a couple of things when I should have been more forthcoming."

"Do you know something about whoever attacked Tommy?"

"No. At least, not directly. It's more about Lisa Sondnes, John. There's a little detail about the story that... I guess I told myself that it wasn't relevant, but I think you should be the judge of that. This probably isn't the right time, but tomorrow I need to tell you about -"

"Where is he?" a voice cried out, and John turned to see Tommy's wife Tracy hurrying toward them. "Where's Tommy?"

"Tracy," John replied, holding his hands up, "we -"

"Where's my husband?" she shouted, stopping and looking round. "I got a call from Carolyn to say he'd been brought here but she didn't know anything else. I need to see him right now."

"He's in the best possible care," Robert told her.

"I'm his wife and I want to see him right now!"

"I think we just have to wait," John said. "Tracy, we need to give the doctors time to treat him and -"

"I'm his wife!" she hissed again, before spotting a nurse hurrying along the corridor.

As soon as the nurse pushed a door open and began to make his way inside, Tracy slipped between John and Robert, forcing her way into the next room before anyone had a chance to stop her.

"Damn it!" Robert snapped, struggling to turn fast enough, leaning heavily on his walking stick. "Someone get her out of there!"

"I'll do it," John replied, making his way to the door and entering the room, then immediately stopping as he saw a dozen or so people working at a bed over by the far wall.

"Tommy, I'm here!" Tracy shouted, frantically trying to get past the doctors and reach the figure in the bed. "Tommy, it's me! Everything's going to be okay, Tommy! I'm here and I won't let anything bad happen to you!"

"We have to get out of here," John said, hurrying over and taking her by the arm. "We'll only be getting in the way."

"That's easy for you to say," she spat back at him. "You're only his boss. I'm his wife!"

"I know that," he replied, trying to stay calm and retain his control of the situation, "but -"

"But nothing!" she shouted, pulling away from him and then pushing several of the doctors aside until she was able to reach the bed. "Tommy, I -"

Suddenly she screamed, stumbling back with a horrified expression on her face. Before John could react, Tracy began to turn, only for her legs to buckle as she fainted. Reaching out, John managed to catch her just in time, and he quickly dragged her across the room and set her down on the floor.

"What the hell was that noise?" Robert asked, finally limping into the room.

"I think she passed out," John replied, checking Tracy's vital signs before getting to his feet.

"The stupid woman should never have come in here," Robert muttered. "I'm sorry, John, I know that sounds harsh but rules are rules for a reason. We can't have civilians shoving their way into situations where they don't belong."

"I know," John replied, turning and looking toward the bed. "She's just so -"

In that moment, two of the doctors briefly moved aside, revealing the bloodied figure on the hospital bed. Horrified by the sight, John took a step forward, watching with a growing sense of dread as he saw two nurses trying desperately to hold Tommy down. Still wearing his uniform, which was torn to shreds in places, Tommy was covered in cuts and bruises that had turned patches of his flesh a dark shade of purple; several of his bones were clearly broken, with bloodied shards poking out through the torn skin around his ribs and the tops of his shoulders. As the doctors and nurses continued to work, however, John could only stare at Tommy's face, where all that remained of the man's eyes were blood-filled pits that were already leaking red trails down onto his cheek.

"Sheriff Tench, is that you?" Tommy gasped, spraying more blood from his mouth as a nurse slipped a needle into his arm, injecting him with a clear liquid. "Sheriff Tench, I'm sorry! I did my best, but he got the jump on me! I'm so sorry I let you down!"

"Dear God," Robert stammered, stopping next to John and surveying the awful scene. "I knew it was bad, but..."

"Sheriff?" Tommy murmured as the injection began to drag him down into unconsciousness. "Sheriff, if you're here, I'm so sorry. I shouldn't have let him get me. I made a mistake. I'm so sorry, I -"

Letting out a gasp, he leaned back just as his entire body began to jerk.

"He's crashing!" one of the doctors shouted, pulling a cart closer and quickly ripping Tommy's shirt open, before placing two pads on the man's chest. "He's heart's stopped! Everyone clear!"

With that one of the nurses hit a button on the machine, jolting Tommy's lifeless body so hard that he shuddered on the bed. The machine nearby was emitting a long, unchanging beep as the doctor prepared to administer another shock.

"I left him there too long," John said through gritted teeth, as he saw the doctors getting to work on the wounds around one side of Tommy's neck. "This is all my fault"

CHAPTER THIRTY

1984...

STANDING IN HER BEDROOM, Lisa held the plastic bracelet in her right hand and slowly turned it around. On one side, her name had been written in neat handwriting; the other side bore the printed name of the hospital. She knew she probably wasn't supposed to still have the bracelet, but she'd managed to slip it into her pocket after it had been removed and for some reason she didn't want to let it go.

Deep down, she was worried she might forget she'd even been to Lakehurst at all.

"Lisa?"

Startled by the sound of her father approaching the door, she quickly slipped the bracelet into her jewelry box. She turned just in time to see Rod stepping into view.

"You're still awake," he said with a gentle smile. "Do you need anything?"

"No, Dad, I'm fine," she replied. "Thank you. You really don't need to fuss. I'm not made of porcelain."

"It must be weird being home, huh?"

"A little." She paused, before swallowing hard. "I'll get used to it. Thanks again for helping me with the application. I'm sorry we had to finish it after dinner."

"Don't be silly, it was a pleasure," he told her. "I know I'm biased, but I think you're going to make a fine veterinarian one day. I don't want to pressure you, but if I end up handing the business over to you one day, I can't imagine it ever being in better hands."

"There's a long way to go before that happens," she replied. "You've still got some good years in you."

"I know," he chuckled, "but you can't blame me for dreaming of hunting and fishing. There comes a point when a man wants to get on with the basic things in life." Now it was his turn to hesitate, as if there was something else he couldn't quite bring himself to say. "It's late," he added, turning to walk across to one of the other doors. "I don't know about you, but I'm exhausted. I bet it's nice being back in your own bed."

"It sure is," she replied, stepping over and pushing the door shut. "Sleep well, Dad."

Once she was alone in the room, she took a moment to glance around. Her father had been right, she *did* feel good to be home, although she couldn't help but notice that her mind still felt very fuzzy. The doctor at the hospital – Campbell, or something like that – had told her that any confusion would lift eventually, but she couldn't help wondering whether she might have forgotten something important. Finally she headed to the window and grabbed the drapes, ready to pull them shut, before stopping for a moment and looking out at the moonlit back garden. She felt strangely restless, as if parts of her memory – of her mind itself – were crumbling away.

After a moment she spotted the shadows of some branches dancing against the far wall. She watched, and after a few seconds she realized that some of the shadows were actually taking the form of a person. Squinting a little, she told herself that most likely she was simply imagining things, yet the person seemed more and more obvious until she began to worry that an intruder was out there in the garden. Holding her breath, she waited for the shadow to fade away, but instead it moved until its hand was raised, and somehow the hand shifted until it looked more like the head of an animal, almost...

A wolf.

Telling herself that she was imagining things, and feeling a faint flicker of pain in the back of her head, Lisa closed the drapes firmly.

***

2004...

The apartment's door swung open and Lisa stumbled through, before pushing the door shut again and leaning back. Breathless and trying not to panic, she slid down until she was on the floor, and already she could feel the memories flooding back.

She remembered the cabin.

She remembered the wolves.

She remembered *Michael*.

How had she ever forgotten? That question seemed absurd now, as if there was no way she could possibly have forgotten one of the most important things that had ever happened in her life. She quickly realized, however, that the answer was so simple.

Lakehurst.

She'd always remembered her time at Lakehurst, at least some of it, but her father had reassured her that she'd merely suffered a little wobble. He'd insisted that everything had basically been fine, and that she'd merely needed a few weeks away to get her head sorted out; now she understood, however, that she'd been sent there specifically so that all her memories of Michael and the wolves could be wiped away. A shudder passed through her chest as she thought of all the times her father had lied to her, and tears began to run down her face as she realized that everything at the cabin had really happened, and that electricity had been used to fry her brain and make it all go away. She had no idea how something so simple could be so targeted, but she couldn't deny that it had worked.

Until now.

"How could I forget all of that?" she sobbed as more tears ran down her face. "How's it possible?"

She'd always known that something was missing in her mind, but she'd assumed that it was nothing important. Now, however, she realized that a defining part of her existence had been wiped away, leaving an empty gap that had somehow haunted her every waking moment. She'd gone through veterinary school, she'd taken over her father's business, she'd lived her life and built a relationship with Wade and done so many other things, all with that gap in her mind refusing to release its secrets. The entire situation felt utterly hopeless and unreal, but as she slowly got to her feet she began to feel a growing sense of anger.

For a moment she thought back once more to the sight of Michael's body shifting and changing, with the bones moving around and realigning to form something inhuman. She remembered the absolute terror that had surged through her chest, and the horrific sound of Michael's skin splitting open as the wolf features had begun to burst through. She realized now that she'd seen a lot of awful things, yet the sight of Michael's body changing had easily been the worst, as if in some way she'd been unable to believe what was right in front of her. She thought back to the expression on his face in those final moments, the hint of helplessness in his eyes, and she remembered how she'd screamed, and then...

And then he must have taken her home.

"Come over here," she remembered him saying all those years earlier. "Hey, Lisa, while we still have time. You know I'd wait forever for you, right?"

All that happiness and hope echoed through to her now, lingering still despite the two decades that had passed.

"I love you," he'd continued. "There, I said it. You don't have to say it back, not if you don't want to. I won't be offended. I just thought you should know that I'll always be here for you. I know things are difficult but I'll wait. And I'll always look after you."

And she'd said those words back to him.

"I love you too," she'd replied, feeling tears welling in her eyes just as she felt more tears now. "Damn it, this is like one of those stupid books I read so much, but... I just know it deep down, in my heart. So why not admit it?"

That had been before he'd changed, of course, and she wasn't sure whether she still felt the same way. Nevertheless, she was struck now by the thought that after twenty years he might still be out there, that for two entire decades she'd been living her life in Sobolton without remembering that he'd even existed. She hurried to the window and looked out at the street, watching the shadows for any hint of his presence, and then she turned and walked over to the middle of the room before looking around. In that moment she began to wonder whether she'd ever truly been alone, whether perhaps in some way he'd always been watching her.

Suddenly she heard someone knocking on the door.

"Who's there?" she called out as she spun round.

She waited, but she heard no reply. Stepping over to the door, she reached for the handle before hesitating for a few more seconds. Her heart was pounding in her chest, and she had to wait for a few seconds to find the bravery she knew she needed, but finally she turned the handle and slowly pulled the door open.

And in that moment, she let out a shocked gasp as she saw the figure standing out there on her front step.

THE HORRORS OF SOBOLTON

1. Little Miss Dead
2. Swan Territory
3. Dead Widow Road
4. In a Lonely Grave
5. Electrification
6. Man on the Moon
7. Cry of the Wolf

More titles coming soon!

Next in this series

MAN ON THE MOON
(THE HORRORS OF SOBOLTON BOOK 6)

As he finally starts to uncover answers about Sobolton's mysterious past, John faces a race against time to prevent another tragedy. Dark forces are closing in, and not everyone in the town wants to risk upsetting the delicate balance that has prevailed for so many years. Soon John finds himself tackling a deadly threat from within.

Meanwhile, Lisa faces a battle of her own. Now that she remembers her past, she has to decide whether to confront the person who drove her to madness. As two worlds start to merge, how can Lisa make sure that evil will fail?

And what does all of this have to do with a dead little girl who – many years later – is willing to burn Sobolton to the ground in order to get justice against her killer?

Also by Amy Cross

**1689
(The Haunting of Hadlow House book 1)**

All Richard Hadlow wants is a happy family and a peaceful home. Having built the perfect house deep in the Kent countryside, now all he needs is a wife. He's about to discover, however, that even the most perfectly-laid plans can go horribly and tragically wrong.

The year is 1689 and England is in the grip of turmoil. A pretender is trying to take the throne, but Richard has no interest in the affairs of his country. He only cares about finding the perfect wife and giving her a perfect life. But someone – or something – at his newly-built house has other ideas. Is Richard's new life about to be destroyed forever?

Hadlow House is brand new, but already there are strange whispers in the corridors and unexplained noises at night. Has Richard been unlucky, is his new wife simply imagining things, or is a dark secret from the past about to rise up and deliver Richard's worst nightmare? Who wins when the past and the present collide?

AMY CROSS

Also by Amy Cross

The Haunting of Nelson Street
(The Ghosts of Crowford book 1)

Crowford, a sleepy coastal town in the south of England, might seem like an oasis of calm and tranquility. Beneath the surface, however, dark secrets are waiting to claim fresh victims, and ghostly figures plot revenge.

Having finally decided to leave the hustle of London, Daisy and Richard Johnson buy two houses on Nelson Street, a picturesque street in the center of Crowford. One house is perfect and ready to move into, while the other is a fire-ravaged wreck that needs a lot of work. They figure they have plenty of time to work on the damaged house while Daisy recovers from a traumatic event.

Soon, they discover that the two houses share a common link to the past. Something awful once happened on Nelson Street, something that shook the town to its core.

AMY CROSS

Also by Amy Cross

The Revenge of the Mercy Belle
(The Ghosts of Crowford book 2)

The year is 1950, and a great tragedy has struck the town of Crowford. Three local men have been killed in a storm, after their fishing boat the Mercy Belle sank. A mysterious fourth man, however, was rescue. Nobody knows who he is, or what he was doing on the Mercy Belle... and the man has lost his memory.

Five years later, messages from the dead warn of impending doom for Crowford. The ghosts of the Mercy Belle's crew demand revenge, and the whole town is being punished. The fourth man still has no memory of his previous existence, but he's married now and living under the named Edward Smith. As Crowford's suffering continues, the locals begin to turn against him.

What really happened on the night the Mercy Belle sank? Did the fourth man cause the tragedy? And will Crowford survive if this man is not sent to meet his fate?

Also by Amy Cross

The Devil, the Witch and the Whore (The Deal book 1)

"Leave the forest alone. Whatever's out there, just let it be. Don't make it angry."

When a horrific discovery is made at the edge of town, Sheriff James Kopperud realizes the answers he seeks might be waiting beyond in the vast forest. But everybody in the town of Deal knows that there's something out there in the forest, something that should never be disturbed. A deal was made long ago, a deal that was supposed to keep the town safe. And if he insists on investigating the murder of a local girl, James is going to have to break that deal and head out into the wilderness.

Meanwhile, James has no idea that his estranged daughter Ramsey has returned to town. Ramsey is running from something, and she thinks she can find safety in the vast tunnel system that runs beneath the forest. Before long, however, Ramsey finds herself coming face to face with creatures that hide in the shadows. One of these creatures is known as the devil, and another is known as the witch. They're both waiting for the whore to arrive, but for very different reasons. And soon Ramsey is offered a terrible deal, one that could save or destroy the entire town, and maybe even the world.

Also by Amy Cross

If You Didn't Like Me Then, You Probably Won't Like Me Now

One year ago, Sheryl and her friends did something bad. Really bad. They ritually humiliated local girl Rachel Ritter, before posting the video online for all to see. After that night, Rachel left town and was never seen again. Until now.

Late one night, Sheryl and her friends realize that Rachel's back. At first they think there's on reason to be concerned, but a series of strange events soon convince them that they need to be worried. On the outside, Rachel acts as if all is forgiven, but she's hiding a shocking secret that soon starts to have deadly consequences.

By the time they understand the full horror of Rachel's plans, Sheryl and her friends might be too late to save themselves. Is Rachel really out for revenge? What does she have in store for her tormentors? And just how far is she willing to go? Would she, for example, do something that nobody in all of human history has ever managed to achieve?

If You Didn't Like Me Then, You Probably Won't Like Me Now is a horror novel about the surprising nature of revenge, about the power of hatred, and about the future of humanity.

Also by Amy Cross

The Soul Auction

"I saw a woman on the beach. I watched her face a demon."

Thirty years after her mother's death, Alice Ashcroft is drawn back to the coastal English town of Curridge. Somebody in Curridge has been reviewing Alice's novels online, and in those reviews there have been tantalizing hints at a hidden truth. A truth that seems to be linked to her dead mother.

"Thirty years ago, there was a soul auction."

Once she reaches Curridge, Alice finds strange things happening all around her. Something attacks her car. A figure watches her on the beach at night. And when she tries to find the person who has been reviewing her books, she makes a horrific discovery.

What really happened to Alice's mother thirty years ago? Who was she talking to, just moments before dropping dead on the beach? What caused a huge rockfall that nearly tore a nearby cliff-face in half? And what sinister presence is lurking in the grounds of the local church?

Also by Amy Cross

A House in London

Having recently moved to London, Jennifer Griffith needs a job. Any job. When she spots an advert for a position as a nanny, she immediately applies, but she has no idea that she's about to be drawn into a nightmare.

Arthur and Vivian Diebold are no ordinary couple, and their son Ivan is no ordinary baby. Horrified by what she discovers, Jennifer is persuaded to stay for at least one night, while the Diebolds enjoy a rare moment away from the house. Before the night is over, however, Jennifer starts to realize that this particular house is hiding some very dark secrets.

A House in London is a horror novel about a girl who dreams of success and fortune in London, and about an elderly couple who'll stop at nothing to achieve their goal.

Also by Amy Cross

The Ghost of Molly Holt

"Molly Holt is dead. There's nothing to fear in this house."

When three teenagers set out to explore an abandoned house in the middle of a forest, they think they've found the location where the infamous Molly Holt video was filmed.

They've found much more than that...

Tim doesn't believe in ghosts, but he has a crush on a girl who does. That's why he ends up taking her out to the house, and it's also why he lets her take his only flashlight. But as they explore the house together, Tim and Becky start to realize that something else might be lurking in the shadows.

Something that, ten years ago, suffered unimaginable pain.

Something that won't rest until a terrible wrong has been put right.

Also by Amy Cross

American Coven

He kidnapped three women and held them in his basement. He thought they couldn't fight back. He was wrong...

Snatched from the street near her home, Holly Carter is taken to a rural house and thrown down into a stone basement. She meets two other women who have also been kidnapped, and soon Holly learns about the horrific rituals that take place in the house. Eventually, she's called upstairs to take her place in the ice bath.

As her nightmare continues, however, Holly learns about a mysterious power that exists in the basement, and which the three women might be able to harness. When they finally manage to get through the metal door, however, the women have no idea that their fight for freedom is going to stretch out for more than a decade, or that it will culminate in a final, devastating demonstration of their new-found powers.

AMY CROSS

Also by Amy Cross

The Ash House

Why would anyone ever return to a haunted house?

For Diane Mercer the answer is simple. She's dying of cancer, and she wants to know once and for all whether ghosts are real.

Heading home with her young son, Diane is determined to find out whether the stories are real. After all, everyone else claimed to see and hear strange things in the house over the years. Everyone except Diane had some kind of experience in the house, or in the little ash house in the yard.

As Diane explores the house where she grew up, however, her son is exploring the yard and the forest. And while his mother might be struggling to come to terms with her own impending death, Daniel Mercer is puzzled by fleeting appearances of a strange little girl who seems drawn to the ash house, and by strange, rasping coughs that he keeps hearing at night.

The Ash House is a horror novel about a woman who desperately wants to know what will happen to her when she dies, and about a boy who uncovers the shocking truth about a young girl's murder.

Also by Amy Cross

Haunted

Twenty years ago, the ghost of a dead little girl drove Sheriff Michael Blaine to his death.

Now, that same ghost is coming for his daughter.

Returning to the small town where she grew up, Alex Roberts is determined to live a normal, quiet life. For the residents of Railham, however, she's an unwelcome reminder of the town's darkest hour.

Twenty years ago, nine-year-old Mo Garvey was found brutally murdered in a nearby forest. Everyone thinks that Alex's father was responsible, but if the killer was brought to justice, why is the ghost of Mo Garvey still after revenge?

And how far will the real killer go to protect his secret, when Alex starts getting closer to the truth?

Haunted is a horror novel about a woman who has to face her past, about a town that would rather forget, and about a little girl who refuses to let death stand in her way.

AMY CROSS

Also by Amy Cross

The Curse of Wetherley House

"If you walk through that door, Evil Mary will get you."

When she agrees to visit a supposedly haunted house with an old friend, Rosie assumes she'll encounter nothing more scary than a few creaks and bumps in the night. Even the legend of Evil Mary doesn't put her off. After all, she knows ghosts aren't real. But when Mary makes her first appearance, Rosie realizes she might already be trapped.

For more than a century, Wetherley House has been cursed. A horrific encounter on a remote road in the late 1800's has already caused a chain of misery and pain for all those who live at the house. Wetherley House was abandoned long ago, after a terrible discovery in the basement, something has remained undetected within its room. And even the local children know that Evil Mary waits in the house for anyone foolish enough to walk through the front door.

Before long, Rosie realizes that her entire life has been defined by the spirit of a woman who died in agony. Can she become the first person to escape Evil Mary, or will she fall victim to the same fate as the house's other occupants?

AMY CROSS

BOOKS BY AMY CROSS

1. Dark Season: The Complete First Series (2011)
2. Werewolves of Soho (Lupine Howl book 1) (2012)
3. Werewolves of the Other London (Lupine Howl book 2) (2012)
4. Ghosts: The Complete Series (2012)
5. Dark Season: The Complete Second Series (2012)
6. The Children of Black Annis (Lupine Howl book 3) (2012)
7. Destiny of the Last Wolf (Lupine Howl book 4) (2012)
8. Asylum (The Asylum Trilogy book 1) (2012)
9. Dark Season: The Complete Third Series (2013)
10. Devil's Briar (2013)
11. Broken Blue (The Broken Trilogy book 1) (2013)
12. The Night Girl (2013)
13. Days 1 to 4 (Mass Extinction Event book 1) (2013)
14. Days 5 to 8 (Mass Extinction Event book 2) (2013)
15. The Library (The Library Chronicles book 1) (2013)
16. American Coven (2013)
17. Werewolves of Sangreth (Lupine Howl book 5) (2013)
18. Broken White (The Broken Trilogy book 2) (2013)
19. Grave Girl (Grave Girl book 1) (2013)
20. Other People's Bodies (2013)
21. The Shades (2013)
22. The Vampire's Grave and Other Stories (2013)
23. Darper Danver: The Complete First Series (2013)
24. The Hollow Church (2013)
25. The Dead and the Dying (2013)
26. Days 9 to 16 (Mass Extinction Event book 3) (2013)
27. The Girl Who Never Came Back (2013)
28. Ward Z (The Ward Z Series book 1) (2013)
29. Journey to the Library (The Library Chronicles book 2) (2014)
30. The Vampires of Tor Cliff Asylum (2014)
31. The Family Man (2014)
32. The Devil's Blade (2014)
33. The Immortal Wolf (Lupine Howl book 6) (2014)
34. The Dying Streets (Detective Laura Foster book 1) (2014)
35. The Stars My Home (2014)
36. The Ghost in the Rain and Other Stories (2014)
37. Ghosts of the River Thames (The Robinson Chronicles book 1) (2014)
38. The Wolves of Cur'eath (2014)
39. Days 46 to 53 (Mass Extinction Event book 4) (2014)
40. The Man Who Saw the Face of the World (2014)
41. The Art of Dying (Detective Laura Foster book 2) (2014)
42. Raven Revivals (Grave Girl book 2) (2014)

43. Arrival on Thaxos (Dead Souls book 1) (2014)
44. Birthright (Dead Souls book 2) (2014)
45. A Man of Ghosts (Dead Souls book 3) (2014)
46. The Haunting of Hardstone Jail (2014)
47. A Very Respectable Woman (2015)
48. Better the Devil (2015)
49. The Haunting of Marshall Heights (2015)
50. Terror at Camp Everbee (The Ward Z Series book 2) (2015)
51. Guided by Evil (Dead Souls book 4) (2015)
52. Child of a Bloodied Hand (Dead Souls book 5) (2015)
53. Promises of the Dead (Dead Souls book 6) (2015)
54. Days 54 to 61 (Mass Extinction Event book 5) (2015)
55. Angels in the Machine (The Robinson Chronicles book 2) (2015)
56. The Curse of Ah-Qal's Tomb (2015)
57. Broken Red (The Broken Trilogy book 3) (2015)
58. The Farm (2015)
59. Fallen Heroes (Detective Laura Foster book 3) (2015)
60. The Haunting of Emily Stone (2015)
61. Cursed Across Time (Dead Souls book 7) (2015)
62. Destiny of the Dead (Dead Souls book 8) (2015)
63. The Death of Jennifer Kazakos (Dead Souls book 9) (2015)
64. Alice Isn't Well (Death Herself book 1) (2015)
65. Annie's Room (2015)
66. The House on Everley Street (Death Herself book 2) (2015)
67. Meds (The Asylum Trilogy book 2) (2015)
68. Take Me to Church (2015)
69. Ascension (Demon's Grail book 1) (2015)
70. The Priest Hole (Nykolas Freeman book 1) (2015)
71. Eli's Town (2015)
72. The Horror of Raven's Briar Orphanage (Dead Souls book 10) (2015)
73. The Witch of Thaxos (Dead Souls book 11) (2015)
74. The Rise of Ashalla (Dead Souls book 12) (2015)
75. Evolution (Demon's Grail book 2) (2015)
76. The Island (The Island book 1) (2015)
77. The Lighthouse (2015)
78. The Cabin (The Cabin Trilogy book 1) (2015)
79. At the Edge of the Forest (2015)
80. The Devil's Hand (2015)
81. The 13th Demon (Demon's Grail book 3) (2016)
82. After the Cabin (The Cabin Trilogy book 2) (2016)
83. The Border: The Complete Series (2016)
84. The Dead Ones (Death Herself book 3) (2016)
85. A House in London (2016)
86. Persona (The Island book 2) (2016)

87. Battlefield (Nykolas Freeman book 2) (2016)
88. Perfect Little Monsters and Other Stories (2016)
89. The Ghost of Shapley Hall (2016)
90. The Blood House (2016)
91. The Death of Addie Gray (2016)
92. The Girl With Crooked Fangs (2016)
93. Last Wrong Turn (2016)
94. The Body at Auercliff (2016)
95. The Printer From Hell (2016)
96. The Dog (2016)
97. The Nurse (2016)
98. The Haunting of Blackwych Grange (2016)
99. Twisted Little Things and Other Stories (2016)
100. The Horror of Devil's Root Lake (2016)
101. The Disappearance of Katie Wren (2016)
102. B&B (2016)
103. The Bride of Ashbyrn House (2016)
104. The Devil, the Witch and the Whore (The Deal Trilogy book 1) (2016)
105. The Ghosts of Lakeforth Hotel (2016)
106. The Ghost of Longthorn Manor and Other Stories (2016)
107. Laura (2017)
108. The Murder at Skellin Cottage (Jo Mason book 1) (2017)
109. The Curse of Wetherley House (2017)
110. The Ghosts of Hexley Airport (2017)
111. The Return of Rachel Stone (Jo Mason book 2) (2017)
112. Haunted (2017)
113. The Vampire of Downing Street and Other Stories (2017)
114. The Ash House (2017)
115. The Ghost of Molly Holt (2017)
116. The Camera Man (2017)
117. The Soul Auction (2017)
118. The Abyss (The Island book 3) (2017)
119. Broken Window (The House of Jack the Ripper book 1) (2017)
120. In Darkness Dwell (The House of Jack the Ripper book 2) (2017)
121. Cradle to Grave (The House of Jack the Ripper book 3) (2017)
122. The Lady Screams (The House of Jack the Ripper book 4) (2017)
123. A Beast Well Tamed (The House of Jack the Ripper book 5) (2017)
124. Doctor Charles Grazier (The House of Jack the Ripper book 6) (2017)
125. The Raven Watcher (The House of Jack the Ripper book 7) (2017)
126. The Final Act (The House of Jack the Ripper book 8) (2017)
127. Stephen (2017)
128. The Spider (2017)
129. The Mermaid's Revenge (2017)
130. The Girl Who Threw Rocks at the Devil (2018)

131. Friend From the Internet (2018)
132. Beautiful Familiar (2018)
133. One Night at a Soul Auction (2018)
134. 16 Frames of the Devil's Face (2018)
135. The Haunting of Caldgrave House (2018)
136. Like Stones on a Crow's Back (The Deal Trilogy book 2) (2018)
137. Room 9 and Other Stories (2018)
138. The Gravest Girl of All (Grave Girl book 3) (2018)
139. Return to Thaxos (Dead Souls book 13) (2018)
140. The Madness of Annie Radford (The Asylum Trilogy book 3) (2018)
141. The Haunting of Briarwych Church (Briarwych book 1) (2018)
142. I Just Want You To Be Happy (2018)
143. Day 100 (Mass Extinction Event book 6) (2018)
144. The Horror of Briarwych Church (Briarwych book 2) (2018)
145. The Ghost of Briarwych Church (Briarwych book 3) (2018)
146. Lights Out (2019)
147. Apocalypse (The Ward Z Series book 3) (2019)
148. Days 101 to 108 (Mass Extinction Event book 7) (2019)
149. The Haunting of Daniel Bayliss (2019)
150. The Purchase (2019)
151. Harper's Hotel Ghost Girl (Death Herself book 4) (2019)
152. The Haunting of Aldburn House (2019)
153. Days 109 to 116 (Mass Extinction Event book 8) (2019)
154. Bad News (2019)
155. The Wedding of Rachel Blaine (2019)
156. Dark Little Wonders and Other Stories (2019)
157. The Music Man (2019)
158. The Vampire Falls (Three Nights of the Vampire book 1) (2019)
159. The Other Ann (2019)
160. The Butcher's Husband and Other Stories (2019)
161. The Haunting of Lannister Hall (2019)
162. The Vampire Burns (Three Nights of the Vampire book 2) (2019)
163. Days 195 to 202 (Mass Extinction Event book 9) (2019)
164. Escape From Hotel Necro (2019)
165. The Vampire Rises (Three Nights of the Vampire book 3) (2019)
166. Ten Chimes to Midnight: A Collection of Ghost Stories (2019)
167. The Strangler's Daughter (2019)
168. The Beast on the Tracks (2019)
169. The Haunting of the King's Head (2019)
170. I Married a Serial Killer (2019)
171. Your Inhuman Heart (2020)
172. Days 203 to 210 (Mass Extinction Event book 10) (2020)
173. The Ghosts of David Brook (2020)
174. Days 349 to 356 (Mass Extinction Event book 11) (2020)

175. The Horror at Criven Farm (2020)
176. Mary (2020)
177. The Middlewych Experiment (Chaos Gear Annie book 1) (2020)
178. Days 357 to 364 (Mass Extinction Event book 12) (2020)
179. Day 365: The Final Day (Mass Extinction Event book 13) (2020)
180. The Haunting of Hathaway House (2020)
181. Don't Let the Devil Know Your Name (2020)
182. The Legend of Rinth (2020)
183. The Ghost of Old Coal House (2020)
184. The Root (2020)
185. I'm Not a Zombie (2020)
186. The Ghost of Annie Close (2020)
187. The Disappearance of Lonnie James (2020)
188. The Curse of the Langfords (2020)
189. The Haunting of Nelson Street (The Ghosts of Crowford 1) (2020)
190. Strange Little Horrors and Other Stories (2020)
191. The House Where She Died (2020)
192. The Revenge of the Mercy Belle (The Ghosts of Crowford 2) (2020)
193. The Ghost of Crowford School (The Ghosts of Crowford book 3) (2020)
194. The Haunting of Hardlocke House (2020)
195. The Cemetery Ghost (2020)
196. You Should Have Seen Her (2020)
197. The Portrait of Sister Elsa (The Ghosts of Crowford book 4) (2021)
198. The House on Fisher Street (2021)
199. The Haunting of the Crowford Hoy (The Ghosts of Crowford 5) (2021)
200. Trill (2021)
201. The Horror of the Crowford Empire (The Ghosts of Crowford 6) (2021)
202. Out There (The Ted Armitage Trilogy book 1) (2021)
203. The Nightmare of Crowford Hospital (The Ghosts of Crowford 7) (2021)
204. Twist Valley (The Ted Armitage Trilogy book 2) (2021)
205. The Great Beyond (The Ted Armitage Trilogy book 3) (2021)
206. The Haunting of Edward House (2021)
207. The Curse of the Crowford Grand (The Ghosts of Crowford 8) (2021)
208. How to Make a Ghost (2021)
209. The Ghosts of Crossley Manor (The Ghosts of Crowford 9) (2021)
210. The Haunting of Matthew Thorne (2021)
211. The Siege of Crowford Castle (The Ghosts of Crowford 10) (2021)
212. Daisy: The Complete Series (2021)
213. Bait (Bait book 1) (2021)
214. Origin (Bait book 2) (2021)
215. Heretic (Bait book 3) (2021)
216. Anna's Sister (2021)
217. The Haunting of Quist House (The Rose Files 1) (2021)
218. The Haunting of Crowford Station (The Ghosts of Crowford 11) (2022)

219. The Curse of Rosie Stone (2022)
220. The First Order (The Chronicles of Sister June book 1) (2022)
221. The Second Veil (The Chronicles of Sister June book 2) (2022)
222. The Graves of Crowford Rise (The Ghosts of Crowford 12) (2022)
223. Dead Man: The Resurrection of Morton Kane (2022)
224. The Third Beast (The Chronicles of Sister June book 3) (2022)
225. The Legend of the Crossley Stag (The Ghosts of Crowford 13) (2022)
226. One Star (2022)
227. The Ghost in Room 119 (2022)
228. The Fourth Shadow (The Chronicles of Sister June book 4) (2022)
229. The Soldier Without a Past (Dead Souls book 14) (2022)
230. The Ghosts of Marsh House (2022)
231. Wax: The Complete Series (2022)
232. The Phantom of Crowford Theatre (The Ghosts of Crowford 14) (2022)
233. The Haunting of Hurst House (Mercy Willow book 1) (2022)
234. Blood Rains Down From the Sky (The Deal Trilogy book 3) (2022)
235. The Spirit on Sidle Street (Mercy Willow book 2) (2022)
236. The Ghost of Gower Grange (Mercy Willow book 3) (2022)
237. The Curse of Clute Cottage (Mercy Willow book 4) (2022)
238. The Haunting of Anna Jenkins (Mercy Willow book 5) (2023)
239. The Death of Mercy Willow (Mercy Willow book 6) (2023)
240. Angel (2023)
241. The Eyes of Maddy Park (2023)
242. If You Didn't Like Me Then, You Probably Won't Like Me Now (2023)
243. The Terror of Torfork Tower (Mercy Willow 7) (2023)
244. The Phantom of Payne Priory (Mercy Willow 8) (2023)
245. The Devil on Davis Drive (Mercy Willow 9) (2023)
246. The Haunting of the Ghost of Tom Bell (Mercy Willow 10) (2023)
247. The Other Ghost of Gower Grange (Mercy Willow 11) (2023)
248. The Haunting of Olive Atkins (Mercy Willow 12) (2023)
249. The End of Marcy Willow (Mercy Willow 13) (2023)
250. The Last Haunted House on Mars and Other Stories (2023)
251. 1689 (The Haunting of Hadlow House 1) (2023)
252. 1722 (The Haunting of Hadlow House 2) (2023)
253. 1775 (The Haunting of Hadlow House 3) (2023)
254. The Terror of Crowford Carnival (The Ghosts of Crowford 15) (2023)
255. 1800 (The Haunting of Hadlow House 4) (2023)
256. 1837 (The Haunting of Hadlow House 5) (2023)
257. 1885 (The Haunting of Hadlow House 6) (2023)
258. 1901 (The Haunting of Hadlow House 7) (2023)
259. 1918 (The Haunting of Hadlow House 8) (2023)
260. The Secret of Adam Grey (The Ghosts of Crowford 16) (2023)
261. 1926 (The Haunting of Hadlow House 9) (2023)
262. 1939 (The Haunting of Hadlow House 10) (2023)

263. The Fifth Tomb (The Chronicles of Sister June 5) (2023)
264. 1966 (The Haunting of Hadlow House 11) (2023)
265. 1999 (The Haunting of Hadlow House 12) (2023)
266. The Hauntings of Mia Rush (2023)
267. 2024 (The Haunting of Hadlow House 13) (2024)
268. The Sixth Window (The Chronicles of Sister June 6) (2024)
269. Little Miss Dead (The Horrors of Sobolton 1) (2024)
270. Swan Territory (The Horrors of Sobolton 2) (2024)
271. Dead Widow Road (The Horrors of Sobolton 3) (2024)
272. The Haunting of Stryke Brothers (The Ghosts of Crowford 17) (2024)
273. In a Lonely Grave (The Horrors of Sobolton 4) (2024)
274. Electrification (The Horrors of Sobolton 5) (2024)
275. Man on the Moon (The Horrors of Sobolton 6) (2024)

AMY CROSS

For more information, visit:

www.amycross.com

AMY CROSS

Printed in Great Britain
by Amazon